Four Wheel *Drift*

For Gerry,
in Calgary.
All the best

Mel Dagg

Four Wheel Drift

Stories: New and Selected

MEL DAGG

THISTLEDOWN PRESS

National Library of Canada Cataloguing in Publication Data

Dagg, Mel, 1941-
Four wheel drift : new and selected stories / Mel Dagg.
ISBN 1-894345-52-5

I. Title.
PS8557.A3F68 2003   C813'.54   C2003-910395-1
PR9199.3.D224F68 2003

Cover photograph by Mark Tomalty/Masterfile
Cover and book design by J. Forrie
Printed and bound in Canada

Thistledown Press Ltd.
633 Main Street
Saskatoon, Saskatchewan, S7H 0J8
www.thistledown.sk.ca

Thistledown Press gratefully acknowledges the financial assistance of
the Canada Council for the Arts, the Saskatchewan Arts Board, and the
Government of Canada through the Book Publishing Industry
Development Program for its publishing program.

ACKNOWLEDGEMENTS

Some of these stories appeared in a different form in *Fiddlehead, Grain, Journal of Canadian Fiction, More Stories From Western Canada, The Best of Grain, The Last Map Is The Heart,* and *What is Already Known.*

"End of Summer" and "Journey Inland" were broadcast on CBC's *Anthology,* and "The Women on the Bridge" was broadcast on CBC's *Alberta Anthology.*

"The Museum of Man" was cited in *The Yearbook of the American Short Story, Distinctive Short Stories,* and has been published in Denmark in an anthology entitled *Linking Levels.*

CONTENTS

SMITTY IS CRAZY. Quite mad. I see that now. It has taken four and a half days locked in the cab of this van with him, listening to his constant ravings as we speed across Canada, to come to this conclusion — definitely crazy.

I'm his assistant. I take photographs, handle equipment, attend to details, arrangements, and like all assistants, feed his craziness. That's my job. That's what I get paid for. Still, it beats working on newspapers. Better to feed the refined craziness of an anthropologist, than the daily hunger of thousands of newspaper readers.

Smitty's craziness is more civilized, more intricate, more complex. It centres around what has become the consuming passion of his life, his mission, his personal fantasy. And the government has granted him unlimited funds to realize that fantasy — The Museum of Man. Five concentrated years of collecting. Totem poles cut down in the Queen Charlottes and shipped to Ottawa, medicine bundles from the prairies. Eskimo carvings, relics, bead-work, and now, his crowning achievement, his, as the Indians would say, coup, Victoria Red Plume. He has heard she is dying, this old woman, the last of the quillworkers, and we have travelled day and night to reach her.

"Preserved, Danny, don't you see? It all has to be preserved, before it's too late, before," his eyes now completely off the road as he turns to me, his voice rising, "before the culture is dead."

"For Christ's sake," I scream, "*we'll* be dead if you don't watch your driving."

He swerves back into our lane just as the transport truck bearing down on us hits the gravel shoulder. Smitty isn't concerned about details. He has his own private vision, his Museum of Man. I close my eyes, trying to catch some sleep as he drones on, reassured by the fact that we're almost there.

Funny though, now that he mentions it, I haven't seen any dying culture, or dead Indians, for that matter. In Kenora, much to the discomfort of the rest of the town, they seemed unavoidably alive. In fact, one of them nearly knocked me over as I walked through the bar door trying to get a little relief from Smitty. Later, on the highway, I tried counting trees, but they began to shrink, smaller and smaller, until there weren't any at all, just Manitoba scrub. Then it was gone and there was nothing, nothing but the inescapable prairie sky. Suddenly I felt small, vulnerable, threatened, dwarfed by a barren nudity that stretched forever, drowning under the immensity of a clear blue flooding sky. It reached down to touch the tips of fence posts, and it reached down to touch me. I shifted uncomfortably in my seat, feeling its presence.

"It all has to be preserved," he said, still overcome by seeing his first live Indians in Kenora. He hadn't noticed the sky. In the evening I pointed the van toward the gigantic orange globe flaring against the western rim of the earth.

He would have shipped them all back to Ottawa, alive, enclosed in his goddamn glass museum cases, if he had the chance. I jammed the accelerator to the floor and hurtled into the consuming flames of the setting sun, thinking maybe seeing the old woman will change him.

The van shakes me awake and I hear Smitty say "we're almost there" as we bump up over the railway tracks and enter the reserve. An old man weaves ahead of the children straggling along the roadside. He is waving at us and I can feel eyes staring out of windows as we rattle down the dusty pothole-pitted road. Finally, Smitty swerves in at a house set apart from the others by a row of poplars and we lurch to a halt in the yard.

We sit staring out through our insect-smattered windshield at the collection of farm machinery, rusted out shells of cars, gas and diesel barrels, tractors, and rolls of barbed wire surrounding us. A whisp of smoke rises from a barrel of smouldering garbage. Three thin half-wild dogs sniff at the base of the barrel, eyeing us nervously. A green plastic garden hose snakes out past the smoking barrel and disappears into an old bathtub overflowing with water. Staring at us dumbly through the distance, a small herd of cattle shiver in the heat as they shake the cloud of mosquitoes clinging to them.

"Well, what are we waiting for?" I ask Smitty. "Let's go," I repeat, grabbing my equipment, opening the door of the van.

"Grannie, there's some men here to see you," calls a small girl, running ahead of us as we pick our way through the yard.

"Yes, I know, child. Now run along and play," a voice answers from the other side of a hedge.

Then, inside the hedge, we see her. She is sitting on a faded red blanket, her quills neatly arranged before her in rows, and as we move toward her it seems she has always been here under this tree, working with her quills, waiting for us. Or maybe she's just squatting on the ground out here because she doesn't want us in her house. And me, I'm starting to wonder what right we have to be here, anyhow.

Watching her long white braids trail down her arched back, her entire body bent in concentration upon the brightly coloured beads, quills, and scraps of leather spread before her, I see that she is much older than I expected. Her brown hands are wrinkled, yet they don't shake. Her fingers move steadily, surely, as she handles her materials. She has passed beyond age. We do not exist. She is oblivious to our presence here, involved in the detail, the creation of a pattern of which we form no part.

"Mrs. Red Plume?" asks Smitty.

"Yes," she answers, not looking up at us.

"We've come from Ottawa," announces Smitty, fiddling with his pen and notepad, "to make a permanent record of you doing your quillwork. My name is Edwin Schmidt, Doctor Edwin Schmidt, and this is my assistant, Danny Stone," he adds, waving at me.

I'm kneeling in front of her, trying to get a reading

on her face, watching the dial of the light meter wave back and forth between the dark brown of her skin and the shining creases catching the sunlight. It's impossible. I'll just have to guess.

"Now, Mrs. Red Plume," continues Smitty, speaking slowly, deliberately, "our research shows that you are one of the last living quillworkers in Canada. It is very important that we record and gather a specimen of your work before it is too late, before . . . " searching for the words he speaks so easily to me, "before it becomes a lost art. Do you understand?"

"Gathering specimens? No. I don't understand. Every summer men like you come to our reserve with cameras, tape-recorders, typewriters. Why? Everything has been taken from us except this land we are enclosed on. There is nothing left here now. What do you want? For years we were told it was wrong to live as Indians, to forget the old ways, the hunt, the Sun Dance, our religion, to farm as whites. But now you come caring only about this single thing, the few sacred remains that remind us of the time when we moved with freedom upon the land. You don't care about us, how we live now."

"But of course we care, Mrs. Red Plume," soothes Smitty, carefully pronouncing her name correctly. "That's why we're here."

"No, you're here because you want this single thing. You do not care whether we are able to put up the thousands of bales of wild reserve grass needed to feed our cattle through the winter. You do not know we can't borrow money on reserve land, like white farmers, to increase our herd or buy better equipment.

13

You do not live on bannock and sell prime beef in Calgary to pay off debts on farm machinery that is already old. You do not live from day-to-day. You do not know. You only care about this single thing. You have taken everything else, and now you want this too. You have no right to ask for this small thing, this little that remains. I do not think you understand that when the legends and myths we speak, telling them through the night, through the years, telling them differently each time, are printed in your children's books, they change, they die. Oh, you will give me a ten dollar bill, or send me copies, but my name is never on the book. And my name is nothing. You are nothing."

"But the civilized world, Ottawa waits . . . " Smitty splutters into the silence as the old woman continues talking right through him.

"My skills at working with quills are a gift, a sacred right given to a chosen few, passed down to only one daughter in each generation. The dyes, the designs, the symbols, none of these are mine. They were given to my grandmother just as she gave them to me. I know which pattern was taken in a coup against the Sioux, which was stolen in a raid on the Crees. I am only the receiver, the last small bead sliding down a waxed thread, fixed forever in a design that reaches back to a time when my people moved freely, shifting across the prairie, following the buffalo. When I hold this small medallion the beads move to tell me their story."

The bright coloured beads flash in the palm of her brown hand, swirling in their spiralled, contained design. She is connected to something outside us, outside herself.

I try to think what that might be, on this reserve, a woman of prestige, an elder, a member of the *Moto-kiks* society, a Holy Woman. As sure as Smitty and I have without ceremony sacrilegiously opened, ransacked, photographed, and framed in glass dozens of them, there's a medicine bundle in that house she will not have us enter, and into which, even as she sits before us, she's already entered, connected to it. My god, while Smitty mumbles officiously and I fumble with my camera, she's rummaging around inside her medicine bundle.

"Do you understand?" repeats Smitty, not understanding, unable to reach her.

A young girl is dancing with the women, weaving a circle, a human mandala of loping, fringed, beaded buckskin, her arched moccasined feet gently touching the prairie with each rhythmic beat of the drum. The smell of fresh smoking meat drips over the fires, drifting through the camp, mingling with the chant of the drummers.

"Yes," she replies finally in a quiet monotone, "I understand," looking up for the first time, right at Smitty, her brown, wizened face expressionless, as if she is looking through him, as if he isn't there. Then slowly, bending in concentration, she begins working with the quills.

She picks up the first red, hollow quill, places it in her mouth, draws it through her teeth, then the next, flattening them one-by-one, drawing them through, placing them over the two strips of sinew, carefully overlapping the quills so they seem one, a continuous band of red, growing slowly at first, now more quickly.

Smitty nudges me, wanting photographs, but I can't get the f-stop right, feeling that medicine bundle pulling, tugging at her back, drawing her out until she is lost in something that has never stopped. Someone else, another woman, directs her hands, draws the quills through her teeth, links them together. And as the strip of red grows, the bond grows, strengthens until they are one, bound together as each of the quills are bound.

The orange embers of the fire flicker across the dark swaying faces of the elders, blending with the humped figures of buffalo painted on the inside of the lodge-skins. The girl watches as the moving shadows of the old people weave among the painted figures of the animals, becoming a single movement. Suddenly, the long grey hair of an old woman shines in the firelight as she leans out of the semi-darkness, into the flames, plunges a willow fork into the fire, and removes on the end of her tongs a bright coal that in the darkness becomes a thin orange line as the old woman traces out her pattern, waving the ember through the lodge, holding it aloft on the end of her willow fork. Four times the bright orange line moves upward to the sky, four times it arcs out of the darkness toward the girl, and four times it moves downward, to the earth. Finally, it is stilled, becomes again a stationary spark on the end of a willow stick. The cord of a leather bag is undone and the dry sweet grass, twisted into a golden braid, is handed to the old woman. Again the spark at the end of her willow tong moves, touching the braided sweet grass until a thin sweet smelling column of smoke begins to rise from the grass. In the silence the girl closes her eyes, breathing in the sweet heavy incense that hangs hovering within the closed cone of the tipi. A hand touches her forehead in the darkness. Quietly the whisper of many voices rises gradually to a soft chant, filling the wind-hushed stillness of the prairie night with prayers.

The pages of Smitty's notebook flap in the hot summer wind as the old woman works on, oblivious to the constant flick of my shutter as I try to freeze each rapid movement, the blur of her brown, wrinkled hands lost in repeated, familiar ritual.

Through air heavy with heat, the buzz of flies, water overflowing from a bathtub, the faint distant drone of a tractor, the low guttural murmur of her voice speaks not to us, but beyond, to her connection.

"Each time I work a quill into place I lengthen the band begun by my grandmother. I hold a quill in my hand and I am with her. We are the two strips of sinew running parallel to each other, joined by the quills that cross over them, joined through time. Now there is only one quill remaining to fit into place, to complete the pattern."

A hot gust of wind lifts the poplar leaves, brushes the grass, bends the dry brown blades almost to the ground. The light keeps changing.

"That's lovely, really lovely, Mrs. Red Plume," says Smitty. "We're just in time."

She holds the quill, turning it between her fingers against the setting sun. She stares at the quill, turning it slowly, as if she doesn't hear him. The thin shaft's sharp tip catches the sun, flaring into the lens of my camera, blinding, bright as the electric white arc at the end of a welder's rod, still it turns.

Tinder dry late September grass crackles under the soft soles of the old woman's moccasins. Beside her the girl walks lightly. These are her favourite days, spent alone with the old woman, apart from the crowded constantly moving life of the camp. For a moment they stand together at the top of the ridge, looking down into the gently sloping small valley. In its lower-most dip, the brown grass is broken by a fringe of green bushes bordering the small creek that slowly trickles, snaking through the centre of the valley. They have waited for this, the day after the first evening of fall frost to lightly brush against the bushes. She cannot contain herself. She begins to run, feeling the seeds of the tall grass flick against her bare legs, the slope of the hill pulling her forward, carrying her faster and faster. At the bottom, breathless, she lies waiting by the creek bed, hearing the faint laughter of the old woman slowly move down the hillside.

The thin, supple branches swoop downward, heavy with the weight of the ripe berries hanging in clusters at their tips. The girl reaches up, her hand closing around the smooth branch. Like blood, the berries fall from the shaking leaves, slowly covering the grandmother's blanket.

The old woman kneels down, scooping a handful of berries into a small buckskin bag, setting them aside for dye. Then the four corners of the laden blanket are tied together and they begin their journey back to the camp. As they slowly climb the hill, both carrying the heavy knapsack of ripe fruit, the girl listens as for the first time she is told of the quillwork; how it is a sacred gift given only to those chosen by the old people; how the fingers of women who work the quills without their blessing become swollen and ugly, so that they are known to everyone, how Lightning, in anger, once blinded a woman who had not been chosen, who attempted to work the quills without permission.

At the edge of the camp the old woman and the girl stop for a moment, resting near the horses. From within the folds of her large dress the grandmother removes the small leather bag. Placing some quills in with the berries, she pulls the draw-cord tight and hands the bag to the girl, telling her to sleep with it.

For two nights the girl tosses in her sleep, shifting uncomfortably, feeling the small lump beneath her body. Then on the third night, startled, she awakes, not feeling the leather bag under her. At her feet sits the old woman. One by one she removes the quills from the bag, rubbing them in bear fat until they shine, scarlet against the coals of the fire.

She is still holding the quills to the sun, staring at the pinpoint, the small concentrated nimbus flaring at its tip. I close the lens opening to cut the glare, taking advantage of her pause to get a portrait.

"What an exhibit this will make for the museum!" says Smitty, looking down at the quillwork resting in the folds of her faded cotton print dress.

"I went to a museum once, many years ago in Calgary, with my husband. It was called a foundation, designed to preserve the history of the West. Crowfoot, the chief who surrendered our land to the CPR, was called a "wise statesman." The RCMP, they said, arrived just in time to save us from ourselves. I have never forgotten the feeling as we stood looking in at objects of our own culture exhibited in glass display cases for whites. Many of them were sacred to our religion. Medicine bundles that could never be recreated, except in a vision, and were only to be opened by their owner, lay undone. I read the neatly lettered card inside the glass case telling of the contents spilling out of the opened medicine bundle. To us, the patterns on the bead-work only lived, moved, if they were worn, the bundles only held meaning for their owners. My husband cursed in our language. A choking dust was settling on everything. We felt death all around us as we left.

"Now I sit here staring west, this almost completed quillwork in my lap, and your museum returns to me. I am beginning to see." She squints into the horizon, pointing two miles away at a yellow school bus.

The highest thing on the horizon, I watch the bus hump across the edge of the earth and disappear, a burnt dot devoured by the blazing globe setting behind it.

"That is the bus returning children for the weekend from the white schools in the city," she says. "Rachel, my granddaughter, will be on that bus. I know that this last quill I hold in my hand must be given to her, as my grandmother gave it to me, not stifled in your glass cases. There is so much to do, so little time. The hide I left soaking in the old bathtub is not yet ready for tanning and in the morning she will come. How the child loves the smell of the soft, smoke-tanned leather as I guide the needle in her hands."

Ignoring her, Smitty licks the flap of a long envelope. He bends forward and picks up the quillwork resting in the folds of her dress.

"But it isn't finished," she says. "Without the last quill in place, the two sinews joined together so the red band narrows to a fine point, it holds no meaning."

"It's perfect, Mrs. Red Plume, just what we want," Smitty says, as he slides the quillwork into the envelope, and seals it.

It is as the old woman leans forward slightly, the lines in her face suddenly sharpening in the camera's frame, that I see for the first time what I should have known all along. That the rapid sequence of film, the record of each movement and detail of her work, shot on the automatic setting, was never quite in focus.

"We've got it Danny. We've done it!" Smitty beams, ecstatic in the cab of the truck, holding the precious envelope, his career, in his hands.

"We don't have anything," I say, for once unable to humour him. "Not even a photograph."

Journey Inland

THEY PASSED THE EMPTY FREIGHTERS, a scattered string of separate, floating, foreign islands filling the harbour as far as Point Grey, propellor blades exposed above the waterline, waiting to dock and be loaded with grain. The tug slipped under the Lion's Gate Bridge, Danny standing on the worn, rear, oiled, wooden deck as the anchored ships receded. Straining against the huge hulls of the freighters they were maneuvering into the docks, the calm morning sea churning into white foam behind their wooden sterns, the harbour tugs seemed even smaller, miniscule. He would not want to work on a tug that never left the harbour, never going for weeks to the Queen Charlotte Islands, or, as they were, to the whaling station. It was his first trip.

In front of him thick steel cable towline scraped noisily across the iron bumper of the stern, disappeared overboard and re-emerged three hundred feet behind at the bow of their barge. An ancient rust-blistered freighter purchased by the owner for scrap, then levelled to the deck and refitted to haul rail cars, the barge bobbed and weaved erratically, jerking out its last life at sea on the end of a towline.

He felt so close, almost level with the sea, separated from it at the stern by only a few feet of freeboard. As they pushed beyond the harbour, passing the last of the freighters, the grey silt discolouration of the Fraser River was slowly, indiscernibly transforming itself into the blue of the Pacific. Beyond Point Grey the sea changed to a slight swell. Only the wind skimming across the surface, sweeping up droplets, broke the contained rising and falling rolling movement. He leaned over the side, wanting to reach out, to touch it. The cold sea spray struck his face. They would be waiting for him in the wheelhouse.

Danny hurried forward along the outer walkway, entering through the galley door, the roar of the diesel vibrating beneath him as he climbed the spiralling stairs to the turret-shaped wheelhouse.

Everything seemed so new, so fresh. It was difficult to believe this was one of the last wooden-hulled deep-sea tugs still working the Pacific Coast. On the forward part of the main deck, cables were piled in neatly coiled stacks. There was no rust. Fresh paint covered every metal fixture. The brass housing encasing the compass, the ship's telegraph, the huge pilot's wheel, even the window he looked out of onto the deck below, shone.

A crumpled looking man with several days growth on a lean weathered face introduced himself as the captain and suggested they flip a coin to decide which deckhand would take his watch and which would take the mate's. Danny watched the coin clatter to a stop on the floor. He got the mate's — midnight to six in the morning and noon to six in the evening. "Guess you might as well go below and settle in," the captain said.

On the main deck he lifted the forecastle hatch, a hole just big enough to squeeze himself and his pack through, and climbed down the ladder to the lower and most forward part of the ship. The removable board that fitted to the side of his upper bunk was to keep him from falling out in rough weather.

"I'd leave it in if I were you," advised the oiler, who had already taken the lower bunk.

In the darkness of the wheelhouse the mate switched on the small light over the map table, checking their course, then flicked it off. Standing at the wheel Danny found himself wondering about the whaling station that was their destination.

Behind the tug, marked only by four dim kerosene lanterns, the barge moved through the sea with them. Rising, falling, it crashed forward with a movement that travelled the length of the long oiled towline, becoming sharp jerky tremors in the wheel encircling his shoulders. Waves crashed into the bow of the tug, spinning the compass points in a luminous green blur he tried to control by coaxing the huge brass wheel back and forth so that the points rolled equally on either side of the median line dropping across the dial of the compass.

He blinked, shaking his head, fighting sleep. The compass points refused to stop, blurred into each other until they were a single glowing meaningless line, fading into darkness as the force of the next wave caught the ship, pitched him forward, and his forehead banged against the top of the brass wheel.

The mate grabbed the wheel, regaining control.

"I'll take it for awhile," he said. "Go below and check the barge."

Outside he clung to the railing as the waves battered against the hull. Water spilled in through the bulwarks, flooded across the deck, then, as the ship pitched, surged out again. He tried to time his run to the stern with the instant when the ship would right itself and the wash begin to run out through the bulwarks, just before the next movement sent it flooding in upon him. He ran, stumbling down the length of the pitching deck, not stopping 'til he gained the winch. At the stern the towline lashed and grated, groaning and scraping across the twelve inches separating the two holding pins.

Alone in the darkness of the rear deck, Danny was ashamed he'd fallen asleep standing up, that when the mate had taken the wheel, he was off course. Behind the tug, dimly outlining the form of the barge, the lanterns seemed to be winking back at him. His feet were wet.

In the messroom he wanted to ask the cook and the engineer about the whaling station but they were absorbed in a game of cards, the cribbage board fastened down to the table with a screw clamp. The engineer dealt. "This time I'll clean you out," he cracked, letting the momentum of the rocking ship slide each card across the table. The cook silently scooped up the cards, unimpressed. Danny got up from the table and returned to the wheelhouse to complete his watch.

All afternoon as they moved through the small islands, the sun casting a glaze upon the smooth surface of the sea, a school of killer whales passed between the islands with them, black triangular dorsal fins emerging, disappearing, then re-emerging as they rolled tirelessly on ahead of the tug. Suddenly one would rise, lifting its huge mass completely out of the water, sea streaming from its slick, black, arcing hump as it broke the surface, shook itself loose, and hurtled into the air, the sun catching, for a brief moment, the pure snow white of its belly before its weight carried it crashing down again into the sea. At dusk the small islands formed dark clumps outlined against the last light of the horizon: floating tufts of trees that never moved, locked in the stillness of the sheltered evening sea. Night reduced them to stationary dots of light momentarily flaring to life as the dial swept the radar screen. The whales were even smaller pinpoints of light, moving satellites gliding through the darkness. In his mind he formed a vision of the whaling station that waited at the head of Quatsino Sound. It was based on a loose, romantic reading of Moby Dick. He had forgotten about the dark flames of the Try-Works.

The cook retreated to his bunk, leaving the crew's supper, The Cape Scott Special, a hastily prepared stew he had named after the last piece of land jutting out from the tip of Vancouver Island, simmering in a single pot secured to the stove with wire fasteners. No one bothered to eat it.

At first there was a rising swell, a steadily deepening, undulating rolling upwards that dropped deeper with each successive swelling wave, until, he thought, a lifeboat would be lost, swallowed in the depths between the heaving breakers. As they approached the tip of the island the waves, steeping higher, broke at the peaks, lashing into whitecaps. The bow of the tug plunged under, burying itself in a wall of sea, then shot up, bringing the ocean with it, spilling onto the decks.

Clutching the railing, his feet apart for support, the mate squinted through the spray running off the windows of the wheelhouse like rain, searching the rough sea for the landmark that would tell him it was time to change course.

"There they are," he pointed at a string of ragged grey rocks that broke out of the ocean's foam, then disappeared as the tug's bow plunged under again. Danny turned the wheel and they began to gradually move from the last shelter of running with the island, crossing over at its tip.

Then the sea broke in upon them. Each wave that crashed against the side of their hull knocked them in closer to the cape, to the rocks waiting in the seething foam. They were so close now he could see three small black puffins perched on the rocks, their bright orange bills thrust out, searching for what the sea might bring. The fin of a mud shark cut through the eddies surrounding the rocks, striking, then disappeared. The mate called for another course change and they rounded the cape, pushed down the west coast of the island by the swelling breakers, searching for the narrow inland passage.

From the deck he could have thrown a stone into the towering cedars that crowded down to the water's edge on either shore. It was more like a river than the ocean, a river that ran inland half the width of Vancouver Island. Around each bend in the narrow channel he expected the whaling station to appear but always there were only the moist glistening rocks, the gnarled twisted roots of the cedars, the dampness of the rain forest dripping, slowly dropping from the ledges into the channel, the sea, as the tug glided inland through the green, silent forest. The gyres of the channel unwound, whirling eddies sliding by as they moved up the narrow passage. Then, rounding a bend, the barge veered out, almost touching the shore. The shaft of sky cut through the forest by the channel opened, the trees on either shore parting as they entered the widening calm of the bay that marked the end of the inlet.

They began to maneuver the barge alongside the tug, replacing one of the heavy holding pins at the stern, tightening the towline until the barge swung around on the pin in a swivelling motion that placed it parallel with the tug. Danny leapt from the tug to the barge's ladder, climbed the rusted hull, and made fast the lines that were thrown to him from the tug. The other deckhand came aboard and the two of them started up the motors in the refrigeration cars where the whale meat would be stored.

Tug and barge moved forward into the bay in tandem. In the wheelhouse the captain's starboard vision was completely blocked by the hull of the barge. He would be docking blind, guided by the instructions radioed to him by the mate from the barge.

From the deck of the barge the details of the harbour slowly enlarged, the whaling station sliding forward through the reddish-brown, lifeless water of the bay. A cluster of shacks curved around the shore, propped up off the beach on thin stilt-like poles, like transitory impermanent visitors that at any moment the forest crowding behind would push into the sea. In the centre of the bay the galvanized tin roofs of two large low-slung buildings slanted up at the sky. A yellow forklift truck bounced down the wharf, a T-shaped platform jutting out into the bay on black, oiled, timber pilings.

It was low tide, a drop of about forty feet. The sky darkened as a cloud of seagulls rose, disturbed by equipment moving on the beach. He watched the circling squawking horde regroup, hundreds of them. Then suddenly, as one, they dropped down again onto the grey mammoth hump slumped on the beach. A heavy suffocating stench, so strong he was forced to breathe through his mouth, hung over the bay. He looked down at the frothing water churning at the side of the moving barge. For the first time he recognized the dark reddish brown discolouration of blood.

The mate and the other deckhand skidded a long ladder down the barge's deck, angling it out at the wharf that in a few seconds would be above them. The barnacle and mussel-encrusted pilings came closer as he waited to climb the ladder and take the lines that would be thrown to him once he had gained the wharf. "Now," signaled the mate, as the wharf hovered above them.

With each step up the rung, Danny felt the unsteadiness of the ladder leaning out into nothing, held up by the two men under him. The distance of the reeking water churning in the backwash between the barge and the wharf closed. The top of the ladder bumped against the wharf and he clambered up the last two rungs. A line was thrown to him and he pulled up the cable tied to it, dragging it down the length of the dock as he searched for a cleat to secure it to. He could feel the slack in the cable already being taken up as the tug and barge began backing off to avoid smashing the wharf. Finally he found the iron anvil-shaped protrusion and bent to begin wrapping the cable around it. But the barge had already begun surging back from the wharf. He was grappling, wrestling with the stiff cable, trying to squeeze a few feet of slack from the unyielding, tugging wire rope. There was none left. There was only the split-second springing tautness as thousands of tons of backward moving barge snapped. His hands froze stubbornly to the cable and he became a small futile figure yanked into forty feet of falling screaming air, ending in the shattering smack of his body striking the surface. Water shot through him as the height of the fall and the weight of his boots drove him deeper into the dark screaming depths. The depth he travelled was drowned in the shock of the fall. Not until he began to rise, straining to retain a last fragment of breath as he ascended upward, was he aware of time.

He broke the surface, sucking the foul air into his lungs, fighting to keep his head above water, his arms and legs churning, flailing in the murky stinking waste of the whaling station as he struggled to tread water. His boots were like lead weights.

On the barge the mate and deckhand crouched, laughing, pointing at him. Why didn't they throw him a line? Christ — he was drowning, drowning in a cesspool, his strength decreasing with each struggling motion to stay afloat and they stood there laughing, pointing to him like a pair of sadistic idiots. The mate leaned out over the barge, arm jabbing at the wharf. "Behind you!" he yelled.

He saw it then, turning his head in the fetid water, facing the wharf. A rusty iron ladder dangled down from the dock, touching the water in front of him. He began slowly stroking toward it; grasped the bottom rung; gathered his strength, and reached for the next. The heavy water streamed from his body as he pulled himself up, his hands slipping in the whitish grey slime left by the rise and fall of the foul water.

The barge moved in again as he reached the top of the ladder and climbed onto the wharf, soaked, exhausted. Danny walked back to the cleat to take the line, his woolen work socks squishing like sponges with each humiliating step. From somewhere behind him a voice called sarcastically.

"Whatsa matter, kid, fall in?"

But he didn't turn around. As he lashed the cable to the cleat, drops of water flew from him with each angry movement. On the dry timbers of the wharf water seeped from his boots, forming small puddles at his feet.

When he finally gained the safety of the tug, he threw away his clothing and stood under the shower, leaving his boots to dry on the deck.

Indians began arriving in the bay to help load the railcars, the insistent drone of their outboard motors drilling through the timbers of the forecastle, forcing him out of his bunk. The mate greeted him in the messroom. "Nothing like the bracing smell of the sea, hey?" He sniffed with feigned pleasure, then, pushing away his uneaten breakfast, his voice dropping in disgust, "smells like a bloody slaughterhouse."

There was nothing to do but wait until the loading was completed, wait and curse the inescapable stench of the whaling station. He decided to go ashore and watch.

Small, huddled together, dark discoloured water licking their sides in little crimson waves that tossed them lightly, the Indian dugouts jerked at the tattered ropes tying them to the lower small-craft wharf. An empty beer bottle bobbed in the water seeping through a small square patch of tin someone had tacked to the inner side of one of the dugouts. The bright enamel of the outboard motor clamped to its stern clashed with the roughhewn weathered adze marks of the carver of the dugout. An oil slick was forming on the surface of the bilge water that leaked through the tin patch as fuel slowly dripped from the inward-tilted motor of the strange unseaworthy looking craft.

He turned and began walking back. The smell of death, of rotting burning whale blubber increased as he climbed the ramp to the larger dock where the barge was being loaded. At the far end of the wharf from which he had fallen, two of the whaling ships, converted corvettes no one had bothered to rename, were docked. Grey blistering naval paint was breaking out into patches of yellow undercoating along their sides. Dull, anonymous, identical except for the still discernible naval numbers painted on their bows, they sat like twin sentinels, darkly overseeing the activity in the harbour. Protruding from the bows, the harpoons, small modern missiles that discharged upon contact, pointed grimly in at the scene on the beach. Flapping in the listless summer wind, the crew's clothing hung drying in the rigging: underwear, socks, stained work clothes fluttering raggedly in the foul air. The crew passed in silence on the wharf, their pallid faces downcast, avoiding him.

Apart, lost in the secret receding knowledge of their race, the Indians toiled under the weight of the heavy sacks of whale meat slung across their bent backs.

Landlocked, tail pointing up the beach toward the forest as if it had swum out of it to die at the edge of the sea, bloated and stinking, a massive animal lay on the shore. A man unreeled a thin cable from a winch, walked with it to the edge of the water, and shackled the cable in front of the V-shaped tail. Someone whistled, the cable jerked tight, and the huge humped whale skidded grotesquely up the beach backwards. The cable slackened and the tail flopped lifelessly in front of a man leaning on a long handled scythe-shaped knife. He pierced the tough greyish-black outer skin, sinking the four-foot blade in up to the handle. Then, holding it in, the man casually, slowly, twice walked the length of the whale. The cable was attached to one end of the cut portion, a signal was given, the cable tightened and a thirty-foot slab of snow-white blubber was gouged out of the whale's side and bounced up the beach.

As piece after piece of the fat was peeled off and skidded up the beach he tried to imagine the moment of contact, the instant when the head of the harpoon, loaded with explosives, found its mark. Muffled, like a depth charge or the tremor of an earthquake, the explosion shuddered, waves of shock spreading through the stricken, humped, thrashing body, emanating outward, absorbed into the sea, finally washing up onto the beach where, in front of him, the seagulls strutted and waddled on webbed feet, pecking and dipping their yellow beaks in blood.

Someone had told him of their sensitivity, of how recordings had been made of them communicating with each other, with men. A chain ramp clanked into motion, slowly jerking the massive, unrecognizable carcass into a shed where Japanese meat carvers waited. The stench of death was everywhere.

They were slaughtering, extinguishing a species, shelving it in tin cans as dog food and he, he was part of it. He breathed through his mouth to avoid the choking odour, but the smell, the feel of death clung to him like the water into which he had fallen. It was on his flesh, as if he hadn't showered. Nauseous, weak, leaning against a building for support, the words of the man on the wharf closed in on him.

"Wattsa matter, kid, fall in?"

He was retching then, doubled over, vomiting. At his feet, blood ran in full open drains down to the sea.

The Blue Heron

HE CUT THE OUTBOARD TO HALF-THROTTLE and the plane of the boat dropped, settling so he could see beyond the bow to maneuver into the bay. As he nosed the small boat in past the buoys, guiding it through the kelp-bed, Danny scanned the cabins strung along the shore. A column of smoke threaded up from one of the chimneys, dissipating into a blue haze hanging in the dark green firs and cedars that climbed the steep embankment behind the cabin. Jennifer was back. He shut off the engine, quickly tilting the outboard so it wouldn't scrape bottom.

Although he'd come in early, the tide was still out. Now he would have to wait for the sea to slowly eat at the outer reef of rock and sand and surge, flooding into the inner tidal pool, before he could be with her.

Routed by the boat's arrival, a feeding mallard beat its wings against the water, struggling into flight. He considered cleaning the two salmon but gutting them over the side of the boat would be awkward. Instead he drifted in the silence of the extinguished engine, the shriek of gulls. He was remembering when he'd first come to the beach.

She met him at the bus depot, driving out through the looping coils of concrete that hooked Seattle to the freeway, past Tacoma, further into the country, finally winding the Volkswagen down a steep narrow dirt road ending in a clearing where vans and old trucks were parked.

"It's this way," she said, pointing out over the cliff.

But by then it was night and all he could see was the dark outline of trees embedded in the side of the steep embankment, and the stairway, 256 wooden steps zig-zagging down the cliff.

"People only bring what they need down here," she said, swinging a backpack laden with food over her shoulders. "It's a long way down."

His hand grasped the rickety wood railing, his feet moving hesitantly down the stairs. At the bottom he made his way along a narrow planked walkway between the cliff and the cabins that lined the seaward side.

It was too dark to see. He felt her hand. She had stopped ahead of him, waiting. "The tide's in," she said.

Along the walkway he heard the gentle lull of the Pacific moving against the timber pilings beneath the beach houses. The smell of the ocean's damp fecundity enclosed him.

The boat drifted, bobbing lightly on the chop until the current nudged it against the reef. Beyond, the blue heron was feeding in the inner tidal pool.

Every day the huge bird dropped from its tree perch, soared across the tidal flat, and settled noiselessly into the pool. He had been vaguely aware of its presence all summer. Now, his last day at the beach, he stared at the stark bluish grey figure that stalked the pool in the fading light, one thin leg raised out of the water, sloping neck, head, beak angled at the pool's surface, eyes probing into the pool. Suddenly the uplifted leg dropped, the coiled unlooping neck thrashed through the pool's surface, and the bird emerged with a silver fingerling clenched between its shaking scissor-shaped beak.

Concentric rings rippled outward from the feeding bird and touched the rim of the pool. The blue heron slowly lifted, crooked his leg, and was as before, poised in stillness.

The tide began to turn. Using one oar as a pole, Danny forced the shallow draft of the boat through the opening in the reef. The hull grated across the rocks and floated free in the inner pool.

Ignoring his presence, the heron remained still, refusing to move as the boat drifted directly before it. Finally the noise of his rowing disturbed the bird into flight. Lifting its long angular frame from the water, the heron passed low overhead, an infinite age in its slow sweeping movement, as if it had always been there and he, Danny, was an intruder.

The dry leather of oarlocks creaked across the silence of the bay as, his back to the beach, he bent to the rhythm of the oars. Small eddies, pushed from each treading dip of his oar blades, lengthened into a parallel twin trail receding behind the moving stern. In the distance the trail diminished into the orange light that bathed the bay, gone like the summer itself: the days with no names in which they had drifted, lost in each other. Now there were none left. He couldn't believe it was over. In another week she would be teaching and he would be in Montreal at the other end of the continent.

The bow of the boat slammed against the shore, lurching him from his thoughts.

He began emptying the boat; rod, tackle box, net, oars, finally the outboard motor. Then, carefully holding them under the gills, he lay the two salmon on the shore.

Crouched at the water's edge, Danny inserted his knife and ran the blade up the length of the salmon's soft white belly. Reaching behind the gills, he wrenched away the entrails in a single piece. It was a male. Overhead the gulls screeched and wheeled, waiting. He lay the limp gutted form on the rocks, rinsed the knife, and began cutting open its mate.

When he had finished cleaning the other salmon he dragged the boat up the shore and stood for a moment, wondering how to store it. At high-tide there was hardly a beach, just the cabin, the sea rising under it.

He tied the frayed rope attached to the bow around one of the timber pilings supporting the cabin. When the boat rose with the tide he would be able to easily lift it up onto the sun porch.

"I got lucky, got two," he called from the kitchen.

There was no answer. He lay the salmon in the sink and walked into the front room, the one facing the sea. Jennifer knelt in front of the stone fireplace stirring the fire with a short blackened shaft of iron.

"It's getting colder out now," he said, rather stupidly.

Her back turned to him, she jabbed at the logs. Glowing red sparks popped onto the hearth and sputtered into tiny specks of black carbon.

"You shouldn't have stayed out so long then," she said, standing up.

She turned toward him, a short woman wearing jeans, a plain shirt, no makeup. In spite of herself she was smiling, glad to see him. Her face, flushed from the fire, showed a slash of thin white scar tissue under her lip from an accident in which she had demolished her car on the freeway. She had been married once but it had lasted less than a year. Now she lived alone, enjoying her freedom, travelling. They had met on a train coming west and had given the summer to each other, lovers running out of time.

Each of them had spent the day in a ritual of meaningless activity — the fire, his fishing, her trip to the city. Out of a sense of survival they were withdrawing, rehearsing ways in which to fill the void each knew their being apart would create. Nothing had worked. At the centre of everything they did was the inevitability that tomorrow he was leaving.

"I'll cook the salmon," she said, hurrying past him to the kitchen.

They were frightened, afraid to face each other. They hadn't sat down to a meal all summer, instead, simply eating from the refrigerator. Now she was cooking.

Everything is getting in the way, he thought to himself, and slipped quietly out the front door onto the sundeck.

Slow withdrawing, imperceptibly changing light slid, shrinking from the bay. He watched it gather into a thin glowing red streak across the western skyline. The light hung just above the horizon, hovering over the ocean with a sudden intense finality, sinking, drowning in the darkening sea. Black, drained of colour, the spiked tips of firs speared the flaring sun slipping behind the point of land on the far side of the bay.

He bent and undid the rope securing the boat to the piling. Light from the cabin window fell through cracks between the boards at his feet, mirrored as wavering ribbons of yellow on the black water rising beneath the sundeck.

Lifting straight up, he strained on the rope until he managed to angle the tip of the boat up onto the sundeck. He stood over the hull, catching his breath, holding the bow so it wouldn't slip back, the stern still floating on the water below. The inside planks were flecked with silver scales as big as his thumbnail. They shone with an oily glimmer in the light from the window. Dark clots of blood had dripped from the gills, staining the cedar slats of the small clinker.

He grasped the inside of the boat and heaving with all his weight, skidded it up onto the sundeck. Slowly lifting one side, he turned it over. He didn't want it to fill with rain in the days to come when it wouldn't be used.

Sea water dripped from the boat, darkening the dry planks of the porch as it traced the shape of the overturned hull into the sundeck. He turned to go inside.

The smell of cooked salmon filled the cabin. She had placed them side-by-side on a platter in the center of the table, heads, tails intact. He couldn't tell the difference between them now, they were identical.

But he had felt the fluorescent orange eggs slip from his hands, the milkiness trail from the membrane of the egg sack, clouding the water white as, crouched with his knife at the shore's edge, he had gutted the second one, the female.

He poked at the salmon nearest him and the flesh fell, flaking from his fork into a thin, moist, pink wafer.

"I hope you like it," she said, absorbed in the details of the meal.

He wasn't hungry. He was thinking about the morning, dreading it.

"Maybe you should just drive me to Seattle, to the bus station," he said. It would be easier that way, an hour's drive, the bus leaving at a predetermined time, easier than her driving him to Vancouver. He wanted it to be easy.

"We can decide tomorrow morning. Forget it for awhile. Not now." She spoke the slow laconic West

Coast drawl he loved to hear. But beneath the mellowness of her voice was a quiet insistence.

She did not resume eating, instead she looked across the table at him. He had destroyed her fragile, carefully arranged dinner.

She deserved better than this, his paralysis, his guilt over leaving. Though they both felt its presence, tomorrow had not, after all, come. She had been trying to tell him something — that they had only this last night.

"I'm sorry, Jennifer." He said it very quietly.

"It's all right." Across the table she grasped his hand, holding it tightly. She was stronger than him, determined to make the best of the time they had left.

They began to reach toward each other with slow unhurried grace, conspiring in the illusion they had all the time in the world.

Each moment was a separate entity in which they lingered, holding it, as they held each other. Time seemed prolonged then.

Afterward, he lay drifting in a kind of spent stasis, half hearing the sound of the tide rising below the cabin's bedroom floor. He shut his eyes, relinquishing himself to the knock, the shove, the lulling, ceaseless finite lap of each wave on the black encrusted timbers.

In the morning he moved about the cabin without awakening her, packing, and then stood by the stove waiting for the coffee water to boil. He stared absently into the kettle and saw the cedar walls, the light-filled windows, curtains, every detail of the cabin shrunk to a small sphere, and in the centre, tiny, distorted in the kettle's round surface, himself.

From the bedroom he could hear her stirring awake. She would be up in a few minutes. She had changed him, transformed him. He no longer knew what he had been, only what he had become. Her touch still bristled on his skin but already he felt the distance between them growing. He had made his choice, he was going back to Montreal. They had been over it all before.

"You know the way," she said, letting him go first.

Stooping under the weight of his backpack, head lowered so that all he saw were his feet, the stairs, he began climbing. With every upward step he took he knew what he was leaving.

"What's the matter?" she called up to him from below.

"Nothing. Just resting," he answered, and slipped the pack from his shoulders. He wanted to see the beach one last time from the height of the cliff's half-climbed stairs.

Round smooth pebbles littered with fragments of bleached white oyster shells, worn, washed, tumbled back and forth by the waves of each incoming tide, sloped down to the perfectly flat expanse of sand, and beyond, the sea. From the distance of the cliff the sandpipers working the far edge of the tide were mere motes. He didn't see the matchstick legs scurrying at the uneven runnelling border between sand and ocean, thin tapered beaks jabbing at sand fleas, small tufted heads nodding with the constant movement of an incurable tic.

"Let's go," he called down to her, and turning his back, resumed climbing.

But Jennifer clutched at the railing. Far below, he could see the heron.

Perched in the last Douglas Fir slanting out over the cliff, the blue heron waited patiently for the pool to form in the dropping tide, to become again the night feeder outside her window. Bent low with the weight of new green closed cones, the bottom branches of firs brushed by his legs as he climbed. Above, like fire in the blue-green mosaic of the hillside, the red twisted limbs of Arbutus raged amid the firs and cedars. Madronnas, she called them, gnarled wildly beautiful ragged trees that grew only by the ocean.

Where was she? he wondered, suddenly realizing he couldn't hear her footsteps below him. He sat down on the stairs, waiting for her.

The dense silence of the rain forest surrounded him. Giant firs loomed, straining for the sky, their massive blackened trunks scaled with age. An Oregon grape bush shook with the scurrying of a small bird rustling its branches, then was still. Hushed, somber as a cathedral, the forest asserted itself.

Sitting there, picking at a sliver of wood in the worn step, watching the woman climb toward him through the grey, coastal morning drizzle, Danny wanted it to be easy.

But it was hard. Jesus, it was hard.

ON HIS BACK, LEGS PROTRUDING from under a broken down green half-ton pickup truck, Danny Stone swore. Using his good hand, he pushed his feet in a crab-like motion, crawled from beneath the truck and standing up, brushed away sharp pieces of gravel and twigs embedded in his back. From the road the hiss of a passing car's tires on the summer blacktop connected him to the continent of highway unraveling in his brain like a black tugging thread.

At his feet, dandelion haloes jigged on the south wind, buffeting yellow jackets from flower to flower among mauve open thistle burrs. Through the distance of the heat haze rising from humped boulders, their black shadows cast across the tidal plain, the roar of the Pacific was diminished to a smooth trickle. Beyond, the surf unfurled into white foam and tumbled back to the sea, a metallic glare of wind wrinkled water shining like a sheet of crinkled aluminum foil stretched to the far horizon.

Danny sucked the blood from his torn knuckle. He didn't have the right wrench, just a crescent that at the last moment, pushing with all his strength against a bolt frozen with rust, had slipped, sending his fist smashing into the undercarriage of the truck.

A driveshaft outside Toronto, then, pushing it on the prairies, a dropped valve that had destroyed an engine, and last night; gearing down to second for a hill, the stick shift suddenly chattering with the rattle of gear teeth and no clutch as he hit the shoulder, beams of the bouncing truck's headlights wobbling into the field in which he now stood. There had been too many breakdowns.

The shadow of an eagle slipped across the bleached silver-grey cedar logs strewn the length of the deserted beach as the bird drifted, waiting for the tide to turn.

Danny threw the wrench into the cab of the truck, switched on the engine and eased out the clutch. The instant it engaged he heard the rending crack of fragmenting steel as two lugs sheared from the plate, exploded through the clutch cover, leaving ragged holes in it. He'd adjusted the clutch too tight and yet, somehow, the truck was jerking forward. He gripped the wheel, coaxing it through the field and up onto the highway.

The faltering truck wound down the coastline of the island, ocean on his left, blur of blue-green balsam and fir on the other side of the road. He kept looking for signs he was nearing a village. Austere, somber, perched in barren snags jutting over every cove, eagles brooded.

He passed the stripped shells of first one and then two more cars rusting at the side of the road, an abandoned cabin, and around an arcing curve in the road a sign perforated with 30-30 bullet holes read:

Queen Charlotte City
Unincorporated

In front of the hospital, hood ajar, an ambulance sank into the lawn on a flat tire. He went to the only service station where a man fumbled through his shop for twenty minutes trying to find a common cotter pin for the clutch, and then, grasping his cluttered bench for support, in a voice slurred with alcohol, asked him to come back some other time.

He'd expected the finality of what it was, the end of the road. But it wasn't like that, this feeling of limbo somewhere between arrival and departure, like being stranded in a small border town.

"Nepal, Morocco, I've been in some strange places but this!" The lean, bearded man's hand swept an arc indicating the curve of the harbour far below the hillside in which the village was set. "This is something else. Been here six months and I still haven't figured it out."

Far below, the pontoons of a seaplane skimmed the still surface of the harbour and became airborne. They watched the single engine plane buzz the treetops of the small fir-tufted island at the head of the bay and drone to an insect-like dot on the ocean's skyline.

"I think I'll go down to the dock," Danny said. "Thanks for showing me around."

"On the islands there are so many ways of going," waved the man and turning, began climbing the hill to the house he'd built on logging company land from driftwood gathered on the beach.

On the narrow wooden sidewalk that ran along the high side of the village's single street, Danny passed three girls from Skidegate gossiping in Haida. He turned to see a massive golden brown dog leaning out over the cab roof of a truck, forepaws thrust up onto the wheel well of the pickup's box, black nostrils flared open, hyperventilating, and as the driver waved, he read, neatly lettered on the truck's tailgate, "Home Grown." Behind the truck, a man with white hair in a thick short braid stepped onto the street, the outline of a psilocybin mushroom embroidered in brightly coloured thread flapping from his faded denim pant leg. On the peeling white painted porch of the hotel, like lizards come out of the shadows into the sun, two drunks smiled lazily, nodding through heavy lidded eyes.

Eighty-five miles off the mainland of the North American continent, the people who had dropped off and weren't going back clung tenuously to the last westerly-most piece of land, beachcombing, bumming, fishing, driving old trucks rigged with winches for Alaskan milling.

To the right of the ramp walkway to the dock's lower floats the broken kicked-in glass door of a telephone booth stood open. He felt isolated, disconnected from the mainland, he wanted to phone someone.

He had thought public telephone booths were for calling cabs and bookies until last year. Shouting to her over the blare of traffic, he had stood in one night after night. It was *not* the next best thing to being there, stamping his feet up and down against the cold Montreal winter; now this sweet summer sea stench wafting through cracks between worn boards. Turning from the booth, he gripped the handrail and made his way down the swaying ramp.

The tide was in, the rhythmic tap of a caulking hammer rang across the water. A woman balanced herself on a gangplank as she bent over a box of provisions she was carrying aboard the Rose Harbour commune boat, an ancient refitted wooden-hulled tug shining under new colours. On the decks of two houseboats pulled by the boat, the landless lounged in the sun, waiting to be towed to yet another cove. Down the dock, men and women whose touching of land was temporary, chipped away rust and brushed bright enamel onto the vessels that were their lives.

Separate from the other boats, a small badly listing trawler leaned into the pier, a steady tap of the caulking hammer echoing from it onto the water. As he walked towards the far end of the pier, the bell-like hammering of steel rang with liquid clarity, accompanying the now audible voice of a man talking rapidly somewhere below deck as Danny stared at the battered hull, listening.

He searched a deck crammed with turnbuckles, rope, fuel cans, winches, the accumulated disorder of a lifetime, trying to connect something on the cluttered deck with the voice below it. There appeared to be no lifeboat.

As if washed aboard by the last wave that had buried the cabin, a rusting anchor was lashed with fraying rope to the base of the mast. There was no name on the bow, unmistakably identifiable by the mottled mixture of colours painted on it over the years. Small square patches of tin and cloth soaked in tar had been tapped and squeezed into the leaking hull from inside of which the man's voice emanated.

Below the waterline, caught in the bilge pump's current, seaweed clung to the hull, trailing a lazy length of green as Danny strained to catch the words spoken within the boat. But it was impossible, an unintelligible monotone jammed rapidly together, holding meaning only for the speaker, answered only by the steady ping of the hammer. Across the clutter of the stern deck a row of polished lures hanging from new gun-metal blue hooks flashed in the sun as they spun on swivels, tinkling emptily in the light breeze like a wind chime. The hammering stopped.

On the forward deck the bald weathered head of a man emerged, climbing from the fo'c's'le hatch, talking to himself. Gaining the deck, oblivious to Danny watching from the wharf, the old man steadied himself, his hand grasping the rigging as he stared into the reflection of his boat wavering on the harbour's moving water.

Doubled over he stumbled sternward, clawing at the wire on which the lures were strung. Finally managing to remove one, he sat slumped over it on some thick rope coiled on the deck. Danny watched his failing hand finally succeed in threading the line through the eye of the lure.

Then, with the instinct of someone caught in a vulnerable moment, he raised his head. As their faces met, Danny, embarrassed, glanced down at the wharf and, feeling it was he who had been caught, turned to walk away.

Danny was at the top of the wharf's ramp when he stopped. Before him, hanging on uncoiled metal wire below a gutted change box was the telephone receiver. Shards of broken glass layered the booth's floor. There was no one to phone. He walked back down the ramp.

"What's with the old man?" Danny asked a tanned brown back crouched over the curve of a blue hull. The man stood up and, not used to talking to strangers, squinted silently at Danny.

"You mean the old Swede?" His face relaxed as he stepped toward Danny, paint brush still in hand, and bending, rested it across an open can of copper paint. "The captain, we call him. Become quite a fixture around here. Harbour's a good home for a week, but man, he's been tied to the end of that wharf for three months now. Every morning he walks up the pier to the fish company's store, buys some supplies, but just never makes it out. Afternoons he climbs that hill." He pointed above the cedar-shaked roofs of the cliff dwellers where Danny had stood earlier with the carpenter. "Nights, he just stands in the cabin, leaning on the wheel. Talks to himself. Too bad, it's the peak of the season. All the boats are out. Knows this coast like the back of his hand. Feels insecure on land, lived on that boat all his life. All he needs is a deck hand, someone to steer, his eyesight's going." He looked directly at Danny. "Anyhow, shape they're both in now, people are wondering who'll go down first."

"How's that?"

"Drinks a bit," he said, turning back to his painting to let Danny know he'd finished.

He stood for a moment, looking at the only fishboat on the dock lean into the pier. He began walking down the wharf toward it, the old man's voice growing louder.

He was pissing off the stern, talking above the yellow stream hissing out from his hunched frame over the seaweed hanging from the propellor when Danny reached the boat. He stepped down onto the deck and standing in rolled-down rubber boots wet with bilge water, buttoned his fly, talking all the while.

Danny strained to make out the rapid blurring of syllables as the old man shuffled across the deck toward him. As he came closer Danny saw that he had no teeth, that was why he couldn't understand, couldn't even lip-read the words. He stood before him in the clothes he lived in, stained woolen Stanfield undershirt, wide police suspenders holding up pants heavy with oil, the man who had unmoored himself from land and now, raving, was its prisoner.

I'll shake his hand, Danny thought, not knowing what to do, confronted, remembering the insecurity, leaning out over the wharf. Across the water the gnarled bony hand tightened hard on his own, blue eyes glittering through him, incoherent vision spouting from his toothless mouth.

And as he looked into the open cavity of the old man's sunken face, Danny seemed to hear the roar of the Pacific in a storm so strong "y'd think it blown from Ja-Ja-" he stuttered, hands thrashing the space in front of him as he tried to seize the word, "Ja-Ja-pan with nothin' stoppin' it but me'n my boat buryin' itself under its heavin' rollers. Comin' to 'round Cape Scott when it hit me late at night just in line with the reef."

Danny knew that reef, had seen the eddied foam churn and seethe around its dark rocks nineteen years ago from the deck of a deep-sea tug. He remembered its name because when they'd come alongside it the cook wired up a stewpot to the stove so it wouldn't slide off and then ran down the flooding deck to his bunk vomiting. The crew, those that weren't too sick to eat, called the meal "The Cape Scott Special".

As the old man continued, the clarity of his speech increased until Danny was able to almost completely understand it.

"I was comin' to on the starboard side when a wave hit me dead on. Big mother banged my head smack against the brass wheel and knocked me on my ass. Must've knocked me out too cause next time I look no matter how many times I open my eyes, the reef, she's on the port side, not the starboard side." He paused and leaning forward Danny saw the scar, the fresh new tissue healing in a small pink slash across the top of this head. "Lucky huh?" he beamed a toothless grin, surprised, amused at finding himself alive, talking to the man standing on the pier.

Lucky, he thought, staring at the scar shining on the head of the man who'd survived his boat turning around in a storm off a reef five ships had gone down on while he lay unconscious on the deck. Lucky, he thought. "Where's your lifeboat?" he asked, and seeing the old man hadn't heard, repeated himself loudly.

Motioning Danny aboard, he crouched to clear a path for him on the deck as he made his way to the rear of the cabin and pushing aside gear and tackle, stood stooped over the only modern and functional looking piece of equipment on the deck; standard government issue, a halved fiberglass drum lying on its side. Grinning, the old man patted the liferaft container fondly.

At least he had *some* sense, Danny thought, wondering why he was still motioning him closer, 'til for some reason he understood that he wanted him to lift off the cover. Maybe, Danny decided, bending over it, he thinks I'm the government safety inspector. Still, he must know that if I remove the cover the rubber liferaft inside will inflate automatically. But looking once more over his shoulder at him, Danny understood he still wanted him to remove it.

He took off the cover and was enveloped by the fumes of hundreds of yeast bubbles popping to the surface between floating hop leaves. This was no liferaft. The air pump — everything — had been discarded but the container in which the brew was fermenting.

From behind, a hand holding a wide mouthed tin mug reached over his shoulder, scooped through thick surface scum, and held the cup up to Danny's face. Grinning, he offered it while Danny stared into the murky brown liquid, preparing for the worst.

It was like Tubourg or Heineken but with a bite. He passed the cup to the old man who quaffed it in a single motion ending with the emptied cup held out for Danny to refill.

"Hits the spot, don't it?" he gasped, wiping his shirt sleeve across his mouth.

Danny nodded. Smooth, very mellow. He sat down on the bulwarks, back to the sea, while the old man rambled on, talking of the ocean, the knock and sometimes shove of sea on the cedar slats of his boat, the loneliness of being kicked by the wind up a channel narrow as a dark river of gyres and whirling eddies unwinding inland through a green silent rain forest. He had come to know it during the storm, the inland passage, every fiord, every cover and channel between the islands and Alaska. He had no charts, only his memory. He'd survived by eating herring spawn freshly laid on kelp, lunging overboard to tear leaves from black bulbs bobbing on the chop as his boat plunged past.

"Not as good as salmon roe. There's a taste you never forget you've had. Ever had it?"

Danny shook his head.

"Somethin' to see, zillions of bright orange eggs the size of beads, milky white trailing in the water from the membrane sac. Funny how when they know their time's up they come back."

"They?" shouted Danny.

"Summer fry no bigger'n yer baby finger when they leave the river they're born in to fatten up for three years in the sea and somehow find the mouth of that same river."

"Isn't it time you went fishing?" Danny shouted.

"Trouble with my eyes. Can't see so good since the accident. Lucy's been takin' real good care of me but I come back to the boat at night because she thinks I've gone fishing. What can I do?" he shrugged, jabbing a finger at his eyes.

Danny sat on the bulwarks, leaning back, listening to the gentle undulance of the Pacific bump the sides of the battered boat. All along the pier, dark green emerald water nuzzled the black mussel-encrusted timbers of the dock. He was so close now he could touch it, feel it. Hand behind his back so the old man couldn't see, he dipped his cupped palm and felt warm water trail through his fingers, sea salt stinging his torn knuckle, cleansing it. It didn't matter now. Nothing could touch him here.

"Got a compass in there?" Danny shouted, pointing at the wheelhouse.

The old man nodded.

"Depth sounder?"

He nodded again.

Danny watched the split dry mast of the trawler creak in the wind, angling askew into the glowing powder blue afternoon sky. Behind it, hovering high above the harbour, encircling the mast, the black outspread perfectly motionless wings of an eagle floated across the faded white remnant of a moon, riding the wind, resplendent in its freedom, playing with it.

"Nice boat ya got here," he shouted, not wanting to repeat the lie.

"Built her out of cedar right over on that beach." He pointed proudly into the green inner cove where the remains of two bows jutted skyward, shallow water lapping at their skeletal ribbing as the rotten hulls sank, year by year, into the sand reef.

Danny sipped his beer. As soon as he could he'd dump the brew overboard. They'd have a better chance that way.

RIGHT AT THE END OF THE WINTER my father bought the land it snowed so heavy he couldn't clear the site so instead he split shakes for the roof.

"Can't wait 'til spring." His breath fogged icily in the damp shed air as he bent over the cedar block, tapping the froe into the grain.

He pulled the handle toward him, gave a sudden snapping twist to the blade, and a cedar shake sprung splitting from the block.

"Hand me down another one, son," he'd say, standing there, waiting for me to pick out a good straight grain.

That was the only time I got to be with him, in the shed after supper. He wasn't driving granddad's old gas-run Diamond T then so he couldn't take me into the woods with him because even though we were still staying in the old man's house on the flats, he wasn't working with him anymore. He was driving for one of the new companies that had come to the island and the company didn't allow that.

"One thing, though," he'd say, "they got plenty of cedar up there."

And while the crew at the siding was loading him up he'd be cutting cedar blocks from the fallen stumps, carefully placing them on the floor of the truck's cab. Then, hands on the wheel, grappling with the weight of the lurching log trailer, on a road so narrow empty trucks returning from the sea dump had to wait on the widened curve of the switchbacks for him to pass, he wound down the mountainside.

He never took his hands off the wheel to eat his lunch until he reached the smooth safety of the highway that followed the coastline through our village. That was my old man, I guess, always in a hurry.

After school I'd watch for him when the big diesel rigs rolled through the village but it was always hard to pick him out because the company trucks all looked the same, yellow, a whole numbered fleet of them. Not like the small family outfits; Kenworths, Macks, Whites, Hayes, all painted different colours, parked in the evening outside their owner's house, long rear trailer perched on the platform behind the cab; spar slanting across the cab roof, name neatly lettered below the chrome door handle: Shelley Brothers, Walter Compton and Sons, and granddad's old red gas driven Diamond T International with no one to drive it now except himself when he could get a contract.

That was something to see, those loaded trucks braking for the hill, swinging wide to make the T intersection at the bottom. They were loaded with logs, those trucks, not spindly little matchsticks they float downriver for pulp in the east, but timber so thick at the butt-end, seven feet across, that three chained together was a load so long the truck and trailer took up both sides of the road, stopping traffic as it creaked around the corner, me standing at the side of the road, no taller than the huge wheels slowly turning in front of me.

I remember that spring how the green-as-sapling new needles broke from the brown scaly buds, brightening the dark blue-green branches of the firs. That June, riding the dirt road home in the old yellow school bus that wound through the scarred, logged-out base of the mountain, I watched the island change and come alive. Between the road shoulder and the rain forest blackberry runners crept out onto the road itself, their small daisy-like petals promising the dark stained sweet juice of summer.

I counted off each day of my last year in school, watching them run by the bus window like the blurred blue-green mosaic of balsam, fir, cedar, and spruce streaming by beyond the clearing at the side of the road, and I thought about how in the fall I'd be working in those same woods with granddad.

Saturdays his pickup would be parked in front of the barber shop or the Rod and Gun Hotel. You'd see him sitting out on the veranda, fists crammed in the bib of his oil stained coveralls, hunched over a table filled with beer, talking with the fallers, buckers, high riggers, and chokers still wearing the sliver-embedded wool Stanfield shirts they'd worked in all week. They talked about how everything on their island was changing; the pace, the ways. Soon, they said, the big new companies would drive them out, there wouldn't be anything left to cut, any room for the small one-truck gyppo logger.

"They got men with no families in camps right in the woods. They don't need high riggers. They got equipment like you never seen, portable spar-trees, telescopic steel shafts mounted on tank treads that can go anywhere, power saws, and most of all, they got government timber leases."

Propped against the side of their bachelor shacks the long two-man handsaws of the Norwegians and Swedes were rusting, idle as granddad's donkey engine sitting on skids in the growing junkyard of equipment behind his house. Like the island my grandfather had known, the forest was receding before the scream of the company's new power saws. Even on Saturdays, as he sat talking about it, those yellow trucks rolled through our village, one of them driven by my father.

He was clearing land for the site by then, burning out stumps evenings and on Sunday. At night, sitting on the beach after we'd finished, he'd tell me about building the house, how there was never enough time. Behind us flames licked under stump roots and below the sound of each incoming wave sifted through small worn pebbles, mingling with voices of fishermen returning across the dark water of the bay.

That was one of the last things we did together, my old man and I. Thinking about it now, I don't even know if he wanted to go, maybe he was just humouring me. But in the evening I'd run along the beach to meet those boats and stand behind the men crouched at the edge of the shore, gutting their catch. I watched them slit open the soft white bellies of salmon, their hands inside the bright pink flesh, lures rigged to rods lying neatly in the bottom of the boat — buck-tails, Tom Macks and the flat spiked wooden blade they swept through the tidal pools for herring fingerlings. He only took me for a few hours one Sunday in the evening, but I remember every minute.

How we skidded the small wooden boat down to the edge of the water, carefully sliding it over pieces of beachwood so we wouldn't scrape its freshly painted bottom. I remember steadying the bow of the boat while he filled it with the tackle box, rod, net, oars; me shoving hard against the bow, the grate of the boat scraping across pebbles as I pushed us from the shore and we floated free, drifting in the bay.

He put the oars in place, began rowing into deeper water, and I started joking with him. "Hey," I said as he bent forward with the oars, "we forgot something."

"What's that?" he asked, breaking his rhythm, oar-blades stilled, dripping over the smooth dark green water.

"Something to kill the fish with once we land it."

"We'll think of something," he replied, dipping the oars.

But it was just a joke. You had to fish for salmon all day, not for just a few hours before the sun went down. Had to be where they ran when the tide turned, with the boats that clustered just beyond the bay at the tip of a small distant island. We were miles from that island with a single rod in the boat. Yet I paid out the line, hoping, counting the strokes between the reel and the first eye.

Each time we spoke, our voices trailed across the calm, limpid sea. He had to be doing something tangible, something where he could see and feel the results. Not this pulling a piece of shiny metal through the ocean in the hopes of attracting a fish. Now there was only the sound of the oars, the steady treading dip of small cupped eddies swirling from the wooden blades with each stroke.

"Guess we might as well call it quits," he called to me, impatient. "It's getting pretty dark, anyway." He stopped rowing and sat erect in the seat, blocking my vision.

And then seeing I wouldn't reel in, he began turning the boat in a wide arc toward the bay so the line wouldn't tangle and I could fish for a few more minutes on the way in. When he'd completed the turn, the rod curved back to the steady light pull of the herring dodger. Then, suddenly it bent and whipped into a lashing living thing.

"Give it some line," he shouted, "some line."

I loosened the tension brake, the reel ratchet whirred in my hands, the rod bending in hard rapid tugs, line screaming out and out. Then the line went slack, the rod straight, lifeless, and I couldn't even feel the weight of the lure. The line began surfacing, floating on top of the water.

"It broke everything, everything," I said.

"Gimme that." He grabbed the rod, cranking in on the reel.

Threading out from the rod, more and more slack line was rising to the surface. At its end, sea streaming from its sides, twisting form shaking into the air as it tried to dislodge the hook, the salmon broke the surface and plummeted down into the water with a smack.

Jesus, it was a big one. It jumped twice more and made a run for the boat, sulking ugly under it.

By this time my father was standing, holding the bent dipping rod above his head, rocking the small boat while I clutched its side and watched the taut, tense line of nylon drawn from the tip of the rod to the water churning around the thrashing brooding salmon, tips of its fins cutting through the surface in tight, tormented circles.

I could see it just beneath the surface, a few feet from the boat, motionless except for the opening and closing of its gills, the wavering tremor of its thick tail steadying itself, gathering strength, mad, crazed with the piercing sting of the small sharp hook that pulled at its powerful jaw.

I slipped the net out onto the water so as not to startle it but the long green shaft of its back lunged under the boat, shooting out the other side as my father swung the rod across the bow. He lifted the rod still higher and for an instant before I slid the net under the salmon, the strain of its weight was on the line. As it thrashed and struggled in the webbing, I felt for the first time the full force of its weight.

Each time I hit it, smashing the hard bone in the top of the head with the oar, its thick tail thumped up and down. And even afterward, while I dipped my hands overboard, washing the blood from them, I could hear the thwack and pump of its tail beat out its life on the boards in the bottom of the boat. We waited, watching, and at last it lay perfectly still. I bent to remove the barbed hook and had to cut it away from the bone with my knife.

It was night when we moved into the bay, our dipping oars churning tiny phosphorescent fragments of light in dark water, that huge silver form lying between us in the bottom of the boat.

We'd gotten lucky, I guess, the coho always run in August. That was the only one we ever caught together, though, because by then the fire season had started and there wasn't time for anything, not even the house.

Every year when the grass got good and dry I set fire to the flats. I burned them down early that summer. It was supposed to kill off the mosquitoes breeding in the sloughs that snaked seaward through the fields below our village, tidal flats from which the ocean had long ago withdrawn. It was supposed to, but the mosquitoes always came back and it was just an excuse for the fun of the burning.

I didn't know then — running through the reedy grass just ahead of the flames, jumping to the safety of the far bank of the slough and feeling the heat blasting across the muddy water — I didn't know that it was our island that was on fire, that it would never be the same again, not then, or later, watching from granddad's porch, sitting with him after supper with that whole two-mile stretch of flats between the highway and the ocean glowing soft red under the black umbrella of the night sky.

Granddad and the other loggers worried that the government would close off the woods because of forest fires. It hadn't rained for nearly a month and it doesn't take long for a rain forest to dry up into nothing but needles and twigs. He'd sit there looking past the tangled coils of wire rope, fuel drums, beyond the donkey engine, past the truck, into the trees beyond the yard. Branches bent low with stubby green cones hanging in heavy clusters, him never saying much, just listening to the cones drop through the still summer air onto the parched ground, but I could tell he was worried. Everything he had was tied up in that equipment, in getting his next contract cut and into the water.

"Yes Danny," he'd say, standing below me in the yard, his back to me, the trees darker now, black scaled trunks towering over him as he stooped to pick up the Vogue tobacco can he used for a spittoon. "What we need is a piss of a good rain."

Climbing those three wooden porch steps worn half through by his spiked logging boots, granddad seemed older that summer, older than his seventy-nine years. "A good rain and a new driver," he'd say. "'Night, son," screen door slamming behind him.

"'Night," I'd call after him as he shuffled through the kitchen, switching off the porch light that left me in darkness.

After he'd gone in I'd sit on the rope swing and drag my feet in the dusty patch of dirt worn under the seat, waiting for him to turn off the light in his upstairs window.

I knew he meant me when he talked about a driver because in the fall I'd be old enough to get a license. My father was driving overtime for the company now, trying to get the logs out before the government closed the woods, getting paid extra for hauling loads at night so I hardly ever saw him now. And it seemed there wasn't much I could do but wait 'til I got my license.

Except I was picking fir cones for pocket money to sell to the buyer from Vancouver who'd come through the village at the end of the season. They sent the seeds to Norway, and other places all over the world I'd never heard of, for reforestation. I never had to go beyond the yard because the trees at the edge of a clearing always yield the most cones. There were never so many cones as that summer, dripping with pitch, hanging in the last, slender, uppermost branches.

I'd take a drink from the well and then get out the sack, hooks, and the rope I stashed behind the wellhouse. I wore running shoes for grip, tying the rope and sack around my waist, shoving the S-shaped painter's hooks in my pockets so my hands would be free. The trees were so big there was nothing to grab at the bottom, just a big branchless trunk, me somehow grasping the limbs above, hoisting myself into them.

After that it was easier, sets of limbs sticking out from the tapering trunk like rungs on ladder. At first I had to test my weight on each branch because the branches at the bottom were brittle and broke easily. At the top, the branches were supple, green, and never broke, but the thin layer of bark skinned easy enough and the white wood shining under it was too wet to grip. I had to be careful not to break the small wart-size pockets of pitch just under the bark because the sap was slippery as grease. It was a two hundred foot drop to the bottom and I never looked down 'til I'd run the rope behind my back, hooked the sack in the limbs, secured my feet in the set of branches below, and tied myself to that thin swaying top.

It didn't take more than an hour before the sack was filled and hanging heavy between the limbs, my hands covered with pitch, fingers stuck together. I couldn't drop the sack straight down because it'd hit the lower branches that extended further and further out from the trunk and the bag would break open, spilling cones all over. I'd start a kind of rocking motion, swaying the top of the tree back and forth, further and further, and the instant I'd arced out the maximum distance, I'd hurl the sack sideways so it'd clear the bottom branches, thumping onto the ground below while I hung on waiting for the top of the tree to stop shaking. Then I'd smoke a cigarette to get my nerve back.

On a clear night you could see everything from there, the sloughs, the fields, the boats beyond, and in the distant sky the dark outline of the mainland I'd never been to. Behind me, the sound of diesel rigs faded down the highway as my father and the other company drivers shifted gears, hauling through the night. Below, the bleached weathered cedar shakes of granddad's roof shone silver in the moonlight. But the ones my father split that spring are still stacked, unused, in that shed on Vancouver Island.

Afterward, standing in that shed, staring at those stacked bundles of cedar shakes, I tried to imagine the house he would have built under them, the house we never lived in.

There were five men in Frank's Barber Shop that Saturday. I never saw it happen. By the time I got there it was just some water that had leaked from failing steam brakes drying on the pavement for a half-mile stretch up the hill to where he'd started braking, and at the bottom of the hill, right at the head of the T intersection, where the barber shop had been, a crowd so thick I couldn't see anything, hanging onto the bars of my bike 'til I couldn't anymore and dropping it clattering to the ground, pushed my way in at the people.

"Somebody got one helluva shave!" a voice cracked behind me.

I hardly noticed the ivory handled razor lying open where it'd fallen from Frank's hand, the spray of white shaving soap flung from the steel blade, blood drying on ragged shards of busted mirror, because I was looking into the bottom of the gulley at the truck that had levelled the barber shop, lying on its side, men climbing all over it with crowbars, that yellow truck with my old man's number on its crumpled caved-in door.

"Waited too long before braking. Guess they just wouldn't hold. Must've been in a hell of a hurry," I heard someone say. Or maybe it was just me thinking out loud, I don't know.

"He just never made it around the corner, that's all, son." It was granddad. "C'mon, I'll drive you home," he said, hand on my shoulder, lifting my bike into the back of his pickup.

Sitting in the cab of his old truck that day he didn't say much. My grandfather had the strangest pickup truck, an old GMC he'd pieced together out of three others. And right where he'd installed the transmission by burning a hole through the floor with a welding torch there was a gaping hole. Sitting in the cab you could look down and see the highway streaming by under your feet, which is exactly what I was doing.

"Don't look down," he said. "You'll fall through."

And it was hard not to. Sometimes I'd see one of those yellow logging trucks turn the corner and I'd get this feeling, like it was him, only it wasn't — same truck, same company, different driver. I couldn't stand that. In the end I couldn't even stand the island anymore. Granddad said he understood. I used my cone money for a stake and he gave me his pickup when I left.

I move around a lot now.

You know, I don't care if he was in a hurry, don't even care about him grabbing the rod from me that day in the boat. I've never even been back to the island since the accident, but yesterday something happened to me.

I was waking up and I heard this sound, the sound of the Pacific pushing sand, pebbles shifting against the sloping shore with each incoming wave, just like when we were fishing or when we used to sit on the beach together, and the sound kept getting louder and louder, like it does when the tide's coming in, and then I really was awake and there was nothing but the empty prairie where I'd been sleeping, but still I could hear that sound, and turning, looking overhead into the trees, I saw it was just the wind lifting the silver undersides of poplar leaves a thousand miles from any ocean, and you know something? I couldn't remember whether I was travelling east or west. I was scared then, really scared.

"Don't look down," I thought. "You'll fall through."

Sunday Evening on Axe Flats

"LET'S DRIVE DOWN TO THE RIVER and see if the saskatoon berries are ready."

It's the old lady, breaking the silence that has fallen over the table.

"Come with us," she says, looking at me.

But there is no need to hurry now as we sit smoking, sipping the last of the tea, the ruddy flush of the day's work in the fields still fresh upon us.

Sometimes when her brown wrinkled bird-like face pierces into me as it did just now, I am frightened, awed by this woman. I've watched her all summer and I can feel the power that moves with her as she pads through the rooms of her house.

I come upon her beading, see her hands, the steady, sure, quick thrust of her needle stab up through the soft, smoke-tanned deerhide, and I know she is oblivious to me, that she has withdrawn into another world. The tiny fragile coloured drops of porcelain move like separate moments sliding down the waxed thread she holds in her worn wrinkled hands. This is her ritual. Each bead in the intricate patterns of her medallions forms a link to her past.

"Our way . . . ," she will say to me, beginning to explain some aspect of her religion with quiet strength.

Then, though she is the grandmother of my child, I feel the separateness, the difference of race and culture bristle in the air between us.

That first night I slept on the couch I could smell it. Thick, heavy hovering incense hanging in the air until it woke me. I saw her then. A dim, wavering, pre-dawn light threading through the window, touching the spiralling smoke rising from her shape. Hunched over the table, the open, beaded leather pouch, the golden braided sweet grass spread before her as she inhaled its sweet burning fragrance.

I turned my back to her, pretending to sleep, trying to give her some privacy in this house cramped with people. But she must have known.

"We burn the sweet grass to forget," she said to me at noon when we came in for lunch.

There are voices in this house, voices of elders, old men with wisdom stamped, furrowed into their faces, women who have grown round, full with age within the loose folds of their long, faded, cotton print dresses. At night they gather in the kitchen, filling it with the rich guttural sound of Blackfoot.

"Our language is that of the animals and trees," she tells me. "That is why you cannot speak it."

And yet I listen to them lean together as one: old people hearing themselves speak the language that binds them together. Then they know and feel they are not contained within this reserve, but are a confederacy of tribes — Blood, Peigan, Blackfoot — related blood lines speaking a single language, running through the reserves of Cardston, Brocket, and

Gleichen. No, not even contained within this country which they know in their hearts wants nothing to do with them, but spilling south over the border, into Montana.

So they wander, driven by the restless nomadic surge of the land that still flows in their blood. Past their tired brown eyes flash the fence posts of ownership, the rich fertile, rolling foothills. Seen from the highway now, through the closed windows of speeding Chevrolets.

There is nothing left to hunt. Except themselves. Their diminishing sense of identity. And this they can only find in the past, in the old ways. So that at the centre of their wanderings, fixed, stationary, a sanctuary they return to again and again, a place where they are sure of themselves in the world from which they are receding, stands this house and the woman who lives in it.

Because she is a Holy Woman, a member of the Gathered Woman's Society, Moto-kiks in Blackfoot.

And if the old people are not here, after her day's work is done, the last child slipped from her arms and dropped onto one of the beds beside the others, she sometimes sits at dusk with me at this table by the window. We watch the flaring sun slowly snuff itself out in darkness. She wraps herself in layers of silence, travelling outside the day, outside herself, waiting. Then, her voice a monotone, she begins drawing the round slow words from within. So that in the silence before she begins I feel it entering the house, gathering in the folds of the medicine bundle that hangs in her bedroom, until she is filled with it, possessed by it, must speak it, is compelled to tell it.

"Above People," she calls them: Sun, Moon, Morningstar; Husband, Wife, Son; the Holy Trinity whose manifestation and servant, *napi*, Old Man, was sent into the void to create the first world, to shape the first people.

And they walked. Felt the touch of grass bend beneath their feet, marvelled as their own shadows moved ahead of them through the first time, guided by the power of their dreams, following and obeying animals, watching as napi showed them endless circles of life.

Beginnings. In time, before treaties, horses, squares. In time, before the soft spot present on the top of each man's head at birth had been closed, hardened by the ages. But in that first time when it still remained open, a receptacle into which, by day, the heavens poured, and at night, the dreams of animals wandered.

And *napi* showed the secrets of his garden to the people. How herbs and roots healed. How men could drive buffalo over cliffs and women could flatten the quills of porcupine between their teeth, dye them with colours that hid in barks and berries, weave them into designs, rub them with bear fat until they shone like the brightness in the days of the men who wore them.

And at the end of that first summer, *napi* gathered the people together at the place where the Bow and Elbow rivers meet. And in that place, when all the people were assembled and a quiet had fallen over the camp, he spoke.

"Soon I will leave you and all this will be yours, east to the Cypress Hills, west to the mountains, north to the Saskatchewan, south to the Yellowstone. It is a good land. Everything you need is here and you will flourish, but," and his arm dropped to his side, for he was tired, "you must always remember the things I have shown you. Keep the soft spots in the top of your head open so you will remain connected to your Creator, *Nato-se*, the Sun. Give the tongues of the buffalo you slay to the Sun. If you kill a white buffalo, give its robe to the Sun.

"Each year at exactly this time you must come to the river and dance for Sun. Boys must watch and learn the dance of the prairie chicken. Old women must lean together, swaying and moving as the buffalo moves. Men, you must dance at the base of a freshly cut poplar pole until you pull from your flesh that part of yourself that is not worthy.

"In this way, through your dancing, Sun will see that your heads are open, that you are connected to Him, and He will strengthen that connection and prevent you from falling. For outside your world is only space. If you sever the connection with your Creator, nothing will hold you. You will fall forever through endless space.

"I am tired now and wish to lie down."

And as he moved among them, the people parted a way for him to pass, for they were filled with his words as they followed him out of the camp to the small hill where he lay down, spreading his arms upon the earth. There were many things they wished to ask him.

In succeeding years, how would they know when the exact time to hold the Sun Dance had come again?

But as they looked down at his motionless body, arms outspread as if they would embrace Sun, they knew that already he was not one of them. That evening, as the sun was setting, a small boy knelt by the still body and marked *napi*'s being, outlining his shape in stones. And in the morning all that remained to remind the people of *napi* were the stones that traced where he had lain. For he had been eaten by the Sun's wife, *Kokomikeis*, the moon.

And the people, slowly at first, hesitantly, first one and then another, remembering his words, began to lift the sadness from themselves in dance. And afterwards they searched carefully among the plants for signs to know this time, so that when it came again they would recognize it and know it as the time of the Sun Dance.

Something she was saying to me, the meaning of it lost in the heavy inertness of the day's labour in the fields, repeating it again now with a strange urgency in her voice. Something about berries.

But the children know, as they begin rummaging noisily through the kitchen for pails, swinging them as they follow her out of the yard ahead of me, climbing into the back of the truck where they jostle each other, waiting for me to get into the cab beside her.

Through the ragged crack in the truck's windshield the road runs past rusted shells of stripped cars parked in the garbage-smouldering junkyard in front of each curtainless shack of the people who will not farm.

What does she see? This woman sitting beside me who so seldom leaves her own house and now wants to be driven to the river. What does she see?

Sullen, ugly, the hungry reserve dogs roam the side of the road, hunting in packs. We pass the slope we've been working: tractors, rake, baler, hay knife propped against a fuel barrel, the few bales that wouldn't fit on our last load waiting for tomorrow.

Now there is only mile after mile of sloping, unrolling, dry brown grassland dotted by a few scattered herds of grazing band cattle. No longer even fence posts to gauge distance as I shift gears and the truck swoops down into the river valley, across the narrow bridge as I swerve off the road into the tall dry grass that bends, flicks and scratches under the floorboards of the bouncing truck.

"Here," she says, pointing out the window at nothing. But I know I am meant to stop, and before I have braked to a halt, the children jump down, running through the grass toward the green fringe of bush that follows the river.

When they finish, they've eaten more than they've picked, holding the half-filled pails up for the old woman to see, their small brown fingers florid with the dark stain of the berries.

"Here Grannie, try some."

"Yes. They are ready," she says, and then turns and walks slowly to the truck, waiting in the cab for the others to finish picking.

Then, when we are driving over the open grassland that begins where the snaking green line of bush following the river ends, she asks me to stop.

Something is wrong. It is as if she has carried the solemn mood that sometimes overcomes her in the house here, into the open prairie. I get out of the truck and walk beside her slow moving figure.

Suddenly, because I have been looking down as I walk, it looms ahead of me, over me. Grey, dead, a few last strips of bark hanging from its sides, cut down, carried here and erected in that other time; a single tree, the pole, juts straight out of the earth, towering over me.

This. And the remains of what was once a sweat lodge, nothing but air now between the thin curving hump-shaped skeleton of willow branches. Only this.

And looking up into the dry sun-baked desolation of the empty hills, I do not see the mass of colour moving behind her eyes. The vast circle of painted lodges, in the centre, societies, converging to witness the summer fulfillment of a woman's spring vow.

Okan Nitaiakitapo: I am going to our dream vision.

As she goes now. Walks beside me and sees the flash of shaking plumage, feels the trembling under-hoof of horses: braves, buckskin, beads glittering in her dark eyes, spreading over the webbed wrinkles of her face.

The waiting of the people, fasting four days until the eyes are hungry for the sight of the *natoas* bundle: paint, prayers wrapped within the closed folds of small animal skins to be passed now, at this moment.

As she had waited all summer for this. Sees what I do not see. Because she is open to the medicine bundle hanging in her bedroom. Each night as she sleeps, the small sacred objects funnel into her until she is one with the generations who have passed its contents down to her.

No. I only see an old woman searching, hear the tinder-dry grass crackle under the soft soles of her moccasins and, as we turn and walk back to the truck, know that it is not some fragment of flesh torn from the breast of the man who last danced, skewered with sinew to this tree, but a ragged shred of bark that dangles and flaps in the empty summer wind.

But seeing the children in the back of the truck with their berries I understand how the people knew it was time for the Sun Dance. I am humbled by this woman, the grandmother of my child. Made small. Her needle arcs out across the land, a thin shaft of steel singing across the continent until it touches me, pierces into me, hooks and pulls me out of cities, threads and draws me back until I am here, sitting beside her.

And I have become the small white porcelain bead fixed forever in the spiralling design of her medallion.

End of Summer

EVERY MORNING, SIX O'CLOCK SHARP, ALL SUMMER the old man woke me, shrill high-pitched screaming steel cutting through my sleep, each triangular pointed blade pressed to the grinding wheel, piercing into my head until the metallic wailing wrenched me from my bed and I fled to the kitchen to escape the noise. I'd sit brooding over breakfast, waiting for the silence of the two long sharpened hay knives to be propped against the barn, and then I'd hear him turn over the old pickup, and by the time I'd finished eating he'd be in the fields, cutting.

There are no roads on the reserve fields, just tough wild grass mixed in with thistles, shrubs, beer bottles, and old pieces of barbed wire fencing that's been down so long he never sees it until it's too late. He'd look at the twigs, branches, and barbed wire poking out of his bales and joke about it, saying how it would give the cattle something to pick their teeth with, how it made them a better breed than the white farmer's, fed on tame hay, but he always went through both knives by the end of the morning, sharpening them again when we came in for dinner.

When I finished breakfast I'd get into the car and drive around 'til I found him, bouncing over the hills, the badger and gopher holes shaking me awake, looking for his tire marks, and then, coming to the top of a rise, I'd see him.

He didn't sit on the tractor, he stood behind the seat, legs apart for balance, his thin body bent forward, swaying with each jarring bump of the rough unfarmed land hitting the tractor's small front wheels, jolting through the steering wheel, wrestling it with both hands, turning to look over his shoulder at the knife behind him, hearing the clatter of the blades. Then when the grass got too thick, or he hit some wood or wire, the blades jamming, and him stopping, throwing the tractor into reverse, then forward again, the blades free and moving so fast he couldn't see them, just hear the rapid scissor-like clicking of a six-foot swath of wild grass falling to the right of the tractor's huge, slow turning rear wheel as he leaned into the rolling pitching movement of slowly cutting his way around the edge of the pond.

I guess that was the best part of the day, seeing him alone like that against the morning sky, before the sun burned into us, and I remember watching, looking down at him that morning from the top of the hill, thinking how he'd moved again, and as I drove down to meet him, how he must have wanted the wet thick grass near the pond.

When he came by on my side he stopped just long enough to help me start the old gas Minneapolis we used for raking. That's all it was good for, raking. It fired, faltered, and I watched him nurse it, first with the choke, then banging the fuel line with a wrench until it sputtered and rattled reluctantly into a smooth, steady drone. Then I was following behind him, the circular steel fingers of my rake turning, barely touching the ground, combing through the cut grass, flinging it out into tidy rows, ready for the baler and the drying sun, the grass so thick there was no need to double windrow, and me losing myself in the rhythm of the tractor, feeling the rolling, flowing hump of the land, seeing the ducks sliding across the still surface of the pond.

And I remember at noon, at the dinner table, him saying how we should go back out in the afternoon and bale because it was getting late in the summer and we were nowhere near the two thousand bales he needed, and in the afternoon

standing on the sheet of shiny worn plywood he dragged behind the baler, watching the ducks drifting on the still, glazed surface of the pond, waiting for it all to lurch forward into heat of heavy bales thumping out the end of that thing so fast I couldn't get one into place before the next was there. The twine was not cutting my hands anymore because it was the end of the summer and I could stack fifty, maybe sixty bales on that plywood now, even though they weren't dry yet, green and heavy so that I couldn't throw the last few up onto the top of the load, just lift them up as far as I could and then bump them hard with my knee and hope they made it, and him never looking back to see how I was doing, every time he turned the whole load leaning out both ways, splitting right down the middle, coming apart into two, high gaping double tiers ready to topple, me running around behind pushing against them hard to hold it together and thinking, leaning into the whole load, thinking how he sure was in a hurry when right then he stopped, jumped down off the tractor, and came running back toward me so fast I knew something was wrong and there was this thing

this thing thrashing and beating its wings across the water, its neck thrust out at us, this crazy thing forgetting even to fly, lunging, weaving across the field on webbed feet, rushing straight at us, and him, just standing there, kicking at the cut grass with his boot and swearing, and then it was above us, right over us, and me afraid to look up but hearing its wings beating, throbbing against the hot empty air, and then him saying very quietly, "Let's call it quits for the day."

It's winter now. In the afternoon we put on our coats, moving quickly across the snow-drifted yard to the corral. The cattle bunch around me as I kick through the ice in their water trough. While they're drinking we shake the snow off the stiff, frozen bales, loading sixteen in the back of the truck, tilting them out over the edge of the pickup's box so there is a small space for me to move down the center. He stops the truck outside the corral, waiting for the last of the cattle to follow us out and I slip the barbed wire loop that serves as a gate latch over the poplar pole and climb into the back of the truck. He drives in a slow, small circle, the cattle following behind us, waiting for me to drop each bale, slipping the knife through the twine, the wild summer grass tumbling loose onto the snow. Every day I've waited, knowing I'll see them in the next bale I open, knowing that they'll be there

barely born, not even feathers yet, just wispy yellow puffs, compressed, frozen now, boxed into a bale of hay, half-formed fragments, the small smashed beaks and severed matchstick legs scattered into a hundred pieces, tumbling slowly out onto the snow, the blades of grass stained with splattered drops of dark brown blood where they hit the baler, like tiny beads the sightless eyes staring up at me out of the snow.

I try not to see them, concentrating on keeping the twine from my opened bundles in the back of the truck. In a few weeks they will be calving, they can kill themselves tangled in a piece of dropped twine. I turn and signal to him through the rear oval window that the truck is empty. His circle complete now, he drives back, leaving the cattle strung out, huddled in small groups around each dropped bale. He will stay up all night not to lose them, the afterbirth frozen solid on the ground by the time he has carried each one into the basement and whittled the mucus from their thin, thawing, trembling hooves with his penknife.

" . . . carries in its veins an antiseptic which was used by the Indians for the healing of sores and ulcers. But its greatest use is for the healing of burns, the burns of the earth itself."

— Annora Brown, *Old Man's Garden*

AFTER HE DELIVERED the horses, Williard found himself glancing through the rear oval window of the truck's cab out of habit, checking, as if they were still there — nothing but air now between the creaking, swaying, wooden slats of the truck's box. Maneuvering the awkward bulk of the empty livestock truck through the congested traffic was getting on his nerves. Finally he pulled into a hotel parking lot on the east side of the city, near the stockyard and slaughterhouses. He needed a beer.

He stood for a moment inside the door, his eyes adjusting to the sudden absence of daylight as he searched through the crowded smoke-filled dimness of the huge bar for an empty table and then sat down near the wall.

Williard sipped his beer slowly, savoring it, watching the hulking white bouncer with the small club lumped in his pocket stalk the aisles between the noisy crowd, and thought absently about the horses.

He couldn't blame the old man. No, not really. No one rode them anymore. Still, they hadn't cost anything to keep except a bucket of oats in the winter whenever he wanted to watch them float across the snowfields and feel them nuzzle against his hand.

His fingers closed around the stockyard cheque in his pocket. They would be able to repair the tractor now, finish the haying — that was the important thing. They couldn't borrow money on communally owned land. Each fall they had to sell off the calves just to meet expenses so that the herd never grew in size. Insurance, his father called the cattle, something to pass on to his sons that would separate them from the cycle of drinking up welfare cheques that had become part of life on the reservation. They ate bannock and relied on shooting the occasional dwindling deer at the river just to maintain their small, static herd. And now they had sold the horses.

He would miss them, the summer coolness of early morning when they cleared the fence, milling noisily in the yard. Jostling each other, snorting as they bumped their flanks against the sides of the outbuildings, their hooves stamping the ground till they sometimes woke him.

A dog food can, that's where they'd end up. For what? For the miserable little herd of straggly cattle they sweated out their lives over. Somehow it didn't seem worth it. He thought again about leaving.

But whenever he thought of leaving he saw his father sitting up every night, waiting for each calf to be born, carrying them into the basement, cutting away the mucus from their hooves. He saw him like that, his old man stooped over a half-frozen newborn black calf, like some small god kneeling to shape its hooves with his jackknife. Or outside in the corral, his huge hands inside a cow, the steamy fog of her breath filling the icy night air as, arms in up to his elbows, he struggled to pull out a stuck calf.

"If we had Black Angus crossed with Herefords this'd never happen," he had said to him, the calf coming out backwards, dead.

He saw him like that, his father trying to breathe life into a dead calf, a ranch, struggling for him, and knew he couldn't leave.

Williard ordered another beer. Nothing had changed in the New Noble Hotel. It was an Indian bar, the kind of place you walked into two years later and saw the same people exactly the way you'd last left them. People with nowhere to go who lived in the bar and when it closed staggered out with as much beer as they could carry and passed out on the floor at an address someone had scrawled on the back of a cigarette package. He had almost forgotten the old feeling of his hands groping through mornings, fumbling for keys, the day, wondering where he was and how he'd gotten there. Now as the stale stifling familiarity began to close in around him he was almost sorry he had stopped for a beer. He didn't want to see anyone.

Drunks staggered by, slumped uninvited at his table, cadged drinks, cigarettes, loose change, then drifted on to some other corner of their blurred vision.

He slid his cigarettes across the table.

"Thanks brother," mumbled the young Blackfoot, his shaking hands attempting to extract a cigarette from the package.

But Williard, hardly noticing him, wasn't listening.

Past the western band making their way to the small square, raised, roped off platform designed to protect the musicians from the brawling crowd, beyond the snack bar where dangling heat lamps puked out fluorescent orange rays into stainless steel food trays, Williard stared through the smoke haze at the girl leaning out over the shuffleboard on the far side of the bar.

Above the beer and noise, hovering over the heads of the crowd in the distance between them, something, the way she moved, her mannerisms, the worn copper rivets shining in her faded jeans pressed against the edge of the shuffleboard, something held him. He put down his glass and watched her get ready for her shot.

Her fingertips spun the round red wheel on the waxed surface of the board, testing. Then in a single motion her wrist snapped, her arm arced out, and twenty feet away her shot exploded the coloured discs clustered at the other end of the board. As the discs spun swirling into the gutter, as she tilted her head up from the cleared board, in that instant of small moving earrings glittering against her brown skin, he recognized, knew her. She's drunk, he thought, but she could always play shuffleboard.

"Well, thanks for the smoke anyway," said the Blackfoot, getting up to leave.

"Huh? Oh yeah. Sure," muttered Williard.

He drank his beer, tried to ignore her, blot her out, but still she was there. She had changed so much that at first he hadn't recognized her and yet, to him, she was still the same.

After awhile, he didn't know how long, she got up to leave and began walking across the bar toward him, into him, until in that crowded place she was all he saw.

Once there had been a sun in her walk that had struck him blind. Now she weaved, steadying herself uncertainly. He knew she couldn't see him. She was the kind of girl you saw on the edge of any Western Canadian city: hitchhiking on the highway, thumb thrust out defiantly, hurling a curse after you as you hurtled on by; nodding off, slumped in a chair in the Queen's Hotel on Saskatoon's skid row; sprawled in a doorway on Hastings Street in Vancouver; or just waiting on a bench in Calgary's bus depot with no ticket and nowhere left to go; the kind of girl you saw anywhere, except for one singular distinction, once she had been his girl.

And he did not see her like that. For the beer had unlocked something he had tried to forget in the physical labour of the farm, losing himself in the cutting pain of baling twine biting into his hands as he threw his weight behind each heavy bale hurled into the truck, willing himself to believe there was nothing before him but the humped rolling flow of land over which the front wheels of his tractor slowly turned, nothing behind but the shuttling thump of compressed boxed bales of wild reserve grass dropping one after another from his baling machine.

Now the memory of her broke, flooding in upon him. He shut his eyes, refused to watch the drunken dishevelled girl who staggered slowly toward him. And like a pinpoint of light enlarging, the aperture of a lens widening until fully open it floods into the unconscious, becomes all light, the shutter's split second all time, the single image all sight, he saw her in that other time, the way he always saw her.

Loosening the plaits from twin black braids trailing down her broad back she slowly wades through the warmth of the still side-pool, her fingers flicking up droplets of spray. Startled minnows dart from her feet and, as she moves her black hair, loose to her buttocks, glitters free for the sun while the river slowly rises through her legs to touch it. Turning once, she looks over her shoulder at him still standing on the shore, and then, pushing herself forward, gives herself to the river. Far out in the depth of the river's surge, her strong brown arms thrust, flash and dip as her hair trails to the river's current. And all the while he is watching her as he slips from the bank beyond the pool at the river's edge, and moves to meet her.

"Can you hold me?" she laughs, as he carries her deeper and deeper, the river's current pulling at his legs, her heavy warmth dripping from his arms.

Across the bar he watched her clutch the edge of a table for support. Now she could hardly hold herself. It had never been the same between them, he had never been able to hold her, to stop her from leaving, not after that night.

He hadn't seen it, though afterwards, as they picked their way through the charred skeleton of the house, she had told him. The first fire truck from the small white town bordering their reserve wouldn't answer the alarm, and the police just sat in their patrol car, watching the house burn, not caring to think or know that anyone was inside. It took both of them to stop her from running into the house, the two of them finally dragging her to the patrol car, pinning her down in the back seat while she kicked and screamed, yelling into their faces over and over, "Don't you know there are people in there?"

"You know damn well why the fire truck didn't come. Because it was on the reserve, that's why," she had said to him, as if that was what she wished to remember, as if seizing on a political issue would somehow absolve, make it easier to live with what she could never forget, that the fire was started from a cigarette, her mother and father suffocating in a stupor from which they never awoke.

"At least they didn't feel anything," she said. She was crying then, and there was nothing he could do.

The following year, one day when they returned to the site, she still hadn't gotten over it, though she had learned to live with it.

"Everyone saw them in the bar that night." She could say it now, accept it.

He watched her tilt the bottle to her lips, draining it.

"Goddam them," she suddenly cursed, tossing the empty bottle into the gutted remains of the house.

The hard edge of bitterness in her voice made it difficult for him to tell whether she meant her parents or everyone outside herself. His eyes dropped to the ground, following the arc of her boot kick angrily at a piece of charred wood. Then he saw them.

Clustered on thin spiked stalks, tiny inverted cups of mauvish red flickered in the wind against the blackened earth on which no other living thing now grew. The charred ground at their feet was ablaze with small bright petals.

"Look Judy," he said, pointing.

"So what," she answered. "It's only fireweed."

He couldn't believe that in the midst of such desolation, in the midst of her raging anger, such beauty could flourish in a wild flower, a weed. Yet it was all around them if only they could see, if only he could make her see.

Even the thin stalks, bent at the top with the weight of small closed buds that hung like beaded drops of blood, were tinged with red. Down the stems, as the bottom buds opened to the sun, their colour changed, lightened, took on the hue of magenta.

It was the colour people of her race so often wear and a slightly different shade of it was reflected in her simple cotton blouse. How he loved the way the florid brightness of her puffed short sleeves gathered in tightly against the deep brown of her bare arms. It was the colour of royalty. It belonged on her, all over her.

He bent down and broke off a cluster of the petals, then another and another, threading the stems through her braids.

"Don't Williard, please, I . . . "

But as he tore the flowers from the ground she saw that he had been seized by a kind of madness, for he was walking backwards, just ahead of her, his arms laden with them, lacing them in her hair, her blouse.

He would make her forget. He would will it. Out of the death of their stifled life on the reservation they would heal, regenerate themselves as the fireweed itself had blossomed from the dead scarred land.

He dragged a small cot, just an iron frame, from the debris of the house. The fire had transformed the colour it had once been painted into ugly yellow-brown heat blisters.

"At least they left us something," she laughed bitterly, looking up at him as she lay on it. "C'mere," she breathed, her arms around his neck, pulling him down.

As the world outside him closed, in that moment before he was lost in her, he saw in the distance the shining flanks of the horses stoop to snatch at the wild grass.

There was a consuming driving energy in her that first startled and finally frightened him, as if she sought to purge what she could not forget in a fury that was as much violence as passion. Only afterward, as they lay exhausted, spent, her quivering warmth stilled beneath him, did he feel the openness, the peace they had once known.

Suddenly she jerked herself free from him. "I don't want anything that reminds me of this place," she said, brushing aside the crushed petals as she began to dress. Already she had begun to talk of leaving.

That morning, the last time he had seen her before she left the reserve, he was fence-mending with his father. She stood in an open doorway across the road watching him tighten and twist the barbed wire in the claw of his hammer 'til it sang with tension. He didn't know how she'd gotten there. She was sleeping anywhere now. She didn't care if he knew.

His father bent and picked up one of the new fence posts — wet green poplars they had cut the day before at the river — dropped it into the posthole and held it in place.

Williard grabbed the sledge hammer and swung it over his head. As she stood watching him he brought the weight of the sledge down full force on the butt of the post, again and again, driving it into the ground.

"Guess that'll keep the strays out," said his father, satisfied, checking the post for tightness, pushing against it with all his weight.

But he wasn't listening. He had to get away and was already stalking toward the truck. "Goin' back to the house to get another roll of wire, Pa." And when he came back with it she was gone.

But that morning, across the road, he had seen again the shore they had swum to and the gulf that now stood between them.

"Hey Williard," she said, slurring her words, "yuh been swimmin' lately?"

She grasped the edge of the table, her head wavering slightly as she looked down at him, as if she couldn't quite get him in focus. As he looked up at her the trace of a hard defiant smile twisted from her lips, then ceased, as if even that was too much to sustain. Beneath her wide black vulnerable eyes shadows dark as bruises had been beaten. She had cut her hair short. Like the old women in mourning, he thought.

He knew then that he had been wrong, that it was his fault. They only had one chance and he had not taken it. They could have found a way, even if they had lived with his family, even if they had lived in the out-buildings, the barn, anything but this. She had nothing after the fire, nothing but her pride, the hard bitter shell into which she had withdrawn. He saw now that even that had been broken.

"Williard, I . . . " she lurched as if to reach the table and instead managed to sit down in the chair beside him. Her hands groped at his neck. Her short, black lacquered hair brushed stiffly against the side of his face. His hands were on her back. He didn't care what she had become. He only remembered what she had been. He wanted her.

"Come back with me, Judy. Stay at our place. You'll feel better."

He felt her stiffen, saw the old stubbornness break over her face. He watched her eyes, so black that the whites had always shown a hint of blue, like porcelain that had now been shattered, for they were etched with tiny veins of red, bloodshot. He had made a mistake, made it sound like charity.

"I didn't mean to," he began, but already she was getting up to leave.

"Yeah, Williard," she said, the angry bitterness rising in her voice as she scraped her chair, "maybe I'm just an ole piece of crow bait but by Jesus I ain't dead yet."

As she turned to walk away he saw for the first time the bored white man leaning against the wall, waiting for her. But he wouldn't watch them leave. Instead he sat rigid, frozen, staring into the smoke-filled emptiness of the bar.

Through the cracked windshield of the truck, the black highway spun out ahead of him. Flattened, splayed, insides exploding onto the asphalt as if plummeted to their deaths, pushed by the hand of a madman from an overhead passing airplane, the shattered remnants of jackrabbits littered the summer prairie highway. He swerved to avoid hitting one. He couldn't stand the dull smack of small bones on his tires. Scavenging crows took flight from the road as he bore down on another unrecognizable clump of fur and blood. What madness burning into their brains caused them to dash from the safety of the fields and hurl themselves onto the highway?

Finally, after what seemed the longest distance he had ever driven, he turned off the highway onto the side road, the pavement becoming a narrow pitted trail of potholes. Behind him the wooden slats of the empty livestock truck rattled like death on the rough reserve road. At last he swung into the yard, gravel exploding under the floorboards, and switched off the ignition.

They would be waiting for him. They worried when he went into the city. But he wasn't going into the house, not yet. He sat in the cab, trying to let the day, her, flow from him. Then he got out of the truck. He would do the chores now, get it over with.

Walking hurriedly past the barn he didn't hear the scratch, the scurrying patter of gophers and the disturbed sudden wing-flutter of small birds in the rafters. The corral gate creaked behind him and he began pumping water into the trough. As he finished filling it, the cattle began to appear in the distance. Strung out, straggling in over the last slope, silhouetted against the salmon-flesh suffusion of the sun's sinking colour, they moved with the slow, deliberate cumulative knowledge of a herd.

Bunching and shoving at the water trough, greenish-brown mud-like liquid spewed stupidly from their rears as they lifted their tails to flick at the swarm of flies that hung over their twitching hides. Ignoring them he stared beyond the trough, the corral, into the dry stubble of the empty hills, where the horses had been. He would never see them again.

But that night he was lurched out of the sleep into which he finally succumbed by the sound of their hooves. Not contained, cramped in the space of their last ride, awkwardly shifting weight as they stamped at the wooden floor of his livestock truck, but riderless, unbroken, they rose through the heat haze of the last hill, their hooves drumming out a steady tattoo on the dry earth.

He was sitting up then, fully awake, reeling in the disorientating darkness of his bedroom. Beating on the fuel barrels in the yard, on the roof, on the sloped cedar shingles of the barn, flung against his windowpane, trickling in muddy rivulets across the dry scale of parched prairie earth, in the loneliness of the place where he lived, he listened to the rain.

JUST ABOVE HER SMALL BUTTOCKS, set in the inward curving cleft of the child's spine, was a mark. "All Indian children have it," explained Dr. Giffen. "It's called a blue mark. They're born with it," reassured the old man, placing his palm on the child's damp forehead, checking her temperature.

It was dark blue, the colour of a deep bruise or welt, almost purple, as if at birth an enormous hand had touched her, pressing in upon the small of her back with crushing strength, setting her apart.

The old man had seen thousands of such marks in his years of practice in the small town adjoining the reserve, but to Fraser and Elaine the child was special.

They had no children of their own, nor had they planned to adopt any. Then a phone call had come from the child's mother. Barely eighteen, unmarried, cut off from the past of her reserve and looking desperately for a future in a crowded city apartment, she found herself in a present defined only by her ten-month-old baby girl.

"Can you take my baby?" she pleaded.

So they knew the child's mother. But more than this, they had known the child's grandparents for years. Summers Fraser helped put up the thousands of bales of wild reserve grass needed to feed their cattle through the long winter. And even during a disastrous year in New Brunswick, they had felt the magic of the old woman's needle pierce up through her smoke-tanned deer hide, arc out at her shoulder, sing through her house, and move out across the land — a tiny shaft of darting steel threading through six provinces, pulling them back across the prairies. They could not resist. That Christmas they had slept on the floor and in the evening sat with the elders silhouetted against the window, watching the winter sun settle in the slow turning dusk in the foothills, feeling the old people's medicine bundle emanate from the folds of small, enclosed animal skins, filling the house with a silence that could be touched.

So for all of them, the child was more than an adoption. It was a gift, given in trust, a merging of two families, an exchange that the nervously efficient social worker who had confronted them with forms in triplicate would never understand.

"It could be complicated, knowing each other like that. Suppose in a few years' time the mother changes her mind, finds herself in different circumstances, and simply decides she wants the child back?" she said.

Fraser watched her pace nervously between the three of them, stopping each time to look over the girl's shoulder at the blank, unmarked forms, the pen idle in her hand. The girl stared at the forms, letting the individual insult of each separate question rise from the paper.

Who is the mother of this child?

_____

Who is the father of this child? (If known).

_____

For what reason are you giving up this child?

_____

The woman loomed behind her. The tone of the adoption forms made her feel she was doing wrong. But why should she? For what? For loving? For opening herself to Willard? For having the baby? She knew what they were thinking but it wasn't true. She loved the child. She had tried for almost a year to look after her, but it was too much for one person. The child deserved better, she deserved a home. They would be good to her. She had chosen them, and yet still she sat, brooding over the unanswered question.

Who is the mother of this child?

"I am the mother of this child," she whispered over and over again.

Welling from within her centre, spreading, shuddering through her body, a wrenching, tearing pain twisted her dark face and filled the room with a moaning, shaking cry.

Fraser never forgot the night before the child had come. It was late and his wife was in bed. He had stayed up to finish painting the crib. He turned off the last light in the house and sat looking out the window.

The prairie sky seemed full of light, grains of moon-star dust caught and reflected in the white snow covering the land. The light seemed to come out of the ground, the white frozen earth, filling the night sky with a deep blue that outlined the giant poplars that surrounded their house. Threading through the tangled gauze of bushes curtaining their window, the light filtered through the glass, settling on the shape of the strange new thing in their bedroom. Even now, at 4:30 in the morning, he could see the rungs, the newly painted bars, the shadow of the crib's shape against the wall. He tried to sleep.

Gifts appeared on his desk. A blanket, clothes so small he couldn't imagine them being worn, a duck that floated in the bathtub. Two nuns they knew in New Brunswick sent a delicate silver chain with the virgin set in a small turquoise stone. Then there was the book. Clad in outlandishly gay colours, grinning from ear to ear in front of the rainbow rising behind them, five absurdly dressed men and a grey cat surrounded the print centred in the clear blue sky announcing *The Pirate's Tale*.

On the first night, Fraser held the child close against him, breaking the winter wind that cut into his back. Her small hands drooped, trailing from the satin border of the thick blanket he held over her head as he dashed her from the truck, through the snow-drifted yard, into the warmth of the house.

He became fascinated by her hands. They were so small, so fragile, and yet so complete. He watched the tiny fists slowly unfold, finger by brown finger, opening like the petals of blossoming fireweed until the small hands were completely exposed, naked, palms upward, fingers sky stretched. Each morning, before dawn, as the darkness slowly rose and dissipated through the sky, the child would awaken and Elaine would quickly take her out of the crib and lay her in bed between them. He awoke to tiny fingers crawling across his face and looked into the child's dark brown eyes.

Then he would carry her to the kitchen and they would look out the window at the snow that had fallen all night, fine and dry, so that instead of settling, the wind whipped it around on the open prairie till it collected in deep drifts and pockets. At their gate the tips of the fence posts barely showed above the snow line and only a few feet further, the ground was barely covered.

Each morning, Fraser shovelled a path to their truck, and each evening, when they returned, it was almost filled in. They were fifteen miles from the highway, one of only two families that drove daily to the city over the unplowed country roads. Like the path, the deep indentations of his tires were almost completely covered when he returned each evening.

One night they stayed in the city late, visiting friends. It was almost midnight when he turned off the highway onto the barely visible road. Fraser fought the wheel, trying to find the morning's tracks, his head bent forward almost to the windshield, eyes fastened on the yellow shafts of the truck's headlights cutting through the shifting, wind-driven snow for a few feet, then snuffed out, lost in the moving drifts. Whispy and hypnotic, the swirling snow enveloped them. They were burrowing through a tunnel that was constantly changing. He blinked his eyes, struggling to stay awake. Between them, limp and content, the child slept.

He was in it, stalled dead by the snow, almost before he saw it, his front wheels locked tight, jammed with packed snow. He tried to spin his wheels in reverse. Nothing happened. The snow was so high he had to force the door open, pushing at it with his legs. It was two feet above the door's bottom ledge. The heater suddenly began blasting cold air into the cab of the truck. He turned off the engine and waded through the snow. Steam instantly enveloped him as he lifted the truck's hood. Tapping the end of his flashlight, a feeble yellow beam settled on the packed snow wedged into a broken radiator hose. Green antifreeze dribbled into the snow.

In the truck his wife sat silent with fear and blame. Fraser knew he had been crazy to take a place so isolated. It was an old quarrel between them, and she was right. He was an irresponsible romantic.

He tried to think. No one else would travel this road tonight. It was too late. Half a mile back at the intersection of two roads, there was a farmhouse. He couldn't remember if the lights had been on. How much time did they have? An hour? Two? Perhaps four if they were lucky. She opened her coat and held the child wrapped in the only blanket against her. He hated to leave them, but there was no choice.

The thought of the two of them huddled in the truck and the freezing cold cutting through his light shoes drove him on. But at the corner there were no lights. A dog barked. There were no cars in the driveway. Then he remembered. Set in from the road, was another house. As he turned the corner he saw through the driving snow the faint glimmer of lights. Someone was still up. He ran, wading in the driveway through snow up to his knees. No one had driven out all day. Would they be able to get through? He hammered on the door. Finally a farmer still dressed in his work clothes peered out at him, then opened the door. Fraser didn't wait to be asked in. He stood in the enclosed back porch, stammering his story. A woman appeared from the kitchen. They seemed amused and only vaguely interested. Huge buckets of milk stood still warm in the room. They were the only dairy farmers in the area, preparing their milk for the morning pick-up. Fraser's half frozen feet shifted up and down. Didn't they understand? His wife and child were still in the truck.

"You'd better drive up there and take a look, Ralph," said the woman.

Waiting for the farmer's truck to warm up, his mind raced ahead to what would happen when they got to his own. With no antifreeze he couldn't risk moving it, and though they were less than five miles from home, the farmer's truck wouldn't make it through the drift either. Skidding out of the driveway and onto the road, the farmer was silent, offering no solution. As they cut through the storm, carefully following the tracks left by his own truck, Fraser envied the self-containment of this gaunt man who hadn't ventured out of his driveway all day.

"Well, I'll be damned! Wonder what the Murdoch boys are doing up at this hour," muttered the farmer. A three-ton livestock truck loomed ahead of them, completely blocking the view of Fraser's own truck.

As they came to a stop, the farmer's headlights picked out a woman hunched against the wind and snow, carrying a small bundle. A burly man held the door open for her, hoisting her by the elbow up onto the truck's foot-step, into the huge cab. Afterward, whenever he thought of a man holding a door for a woman, he remembered not elegance and formality, but the vivid reality of that night, and that man.

"Well, I'll leave you here," said the farmer. "Looks like you're in good hands."

"Thanks, Mister . . . ?"

"Evans. Ralph Evans," replied the farmer, already shifting into reverse as Fraser opened the door of the truck to get out.

"Thanks again, Mr. Evans."

Fraser crowded into the cab of the livestock truck. With the two men, his wife and child in the cab, he stared out through the snow at his crippled truck blocking their path. The child, who had slept through it all, awoke, looking saucily up at her rescuers, unaware of what had taken place.

The two brothers had been at a bull sale in the city and stayed late, explained the driver. The truck rocked as the large animal, confined in a box of wooden slats behind the cab, shifted its weight. Beside him, Fraser felt his wife tense as he watched some white rum in a bottle lying on the dash slosh lazily to the movement of the huge bull behind them. When they were finally home, she told him they had parked and waited a full ten minutes before asking her to sit in their truck. They were rough young men, at home working their father's ranch, shy and gentle away from it, embarrassed by their drunkenness.

"Care for a drink?" giggled the red faced man next to the driver as the truck lurched around Fraser's stranded pickup, its huge wheels easily clearing the snowdrift that had stopped Fraser. They passed the bottle and the warm liquid moved inside him. He rubbed his feet, conscious now of their existance as his circulation returned. They'd have to return and work for hours to free his truck and tow it home, but they were safe. The child was the reason for that. He was sure of it. He'd discuss it with the child's grandmother when he got the chance.

On the weekend, a Chinook interrupted the cold spell, gusts of warm Pacific Ocean air broke through the Rockies, drifting out through the foothills and onto the prairies. The warm air momentarily thawed the top layer of snow, before it froze again, the prairie glittering, gleaming with a metallic, brittle, shining surface, brilliant in the cold February sun. As if a hand had shaped and rounded the edges of the snowdrifts, the ice glaze smoothed the sharp corners of the four foot wall of snow that marked the edge of the road. Fraser squinted in the bright reflected sun as he drove along the snow covered country road, the child seated beside him. Together they would travel east, to the reserve, and visit the grandmother.

The truck's radio picked up the unmistakable bass line of Motown as the Temptations began to sing Smokey Robinson's "My Girl." Fraser was singing, bending down and buzzing the words into her ear as the child ecstatically weaved her head to the rhythm filling the enclosed truck cab.

To her, every object, each event, each separate note, even of the chords, was apprehended with the awe and wonder of its newness. She brought into a world that had become, for him, false and filled with lies, the freshness of her vision. The poet was right: "The child is father of the man." She had kindled in him a kind of rebirth. He began to take nothing for granted, to see as she saw, to become like her. He looked down at her, so small she had to strain to see, to gain an eye level at the bottom ledge of the truck's window, and he was overcome, her beauty destroyed him, shrank him, until he too became small, humble, sensible of the minuteness of his place in a world he was seeing for the first time.

As they passed the Murdoch's place tiny birds, black against the blazing sun, lined the length of the barn's rooftop. The song on the truck radio would never end. They would never reach the highway. Together, they would drive forever, drifting, floating like the pirates in her book.

The words of the song were still with him as the old woman padded in and out of her kitchen, brewing more tea, listening to his story. Finally, she sat down.

He watched the creased lines in her wrinkled brown face and knew that she understood.

Day-by-day Fraser and the child watched as the snow melted, at first so slowly they could hardly see the change. Then ground animals began to appear, lost and bewildered. The jackrabbits shed their winter camouflage. At night, mottled with brown and remaining streaks of white, they were startled by his headlights and ran in panic ahead of the truck before leaping the ditch and disappearing into the dark fields. Cattle were let out of corrals and stables. Bunched together, their necks straining out through strands of barbed wire, they reached for last year's grass on the other side of the fence. Behind them, small calves, still weak on their spindly legs, stood waiting their turn. In the stillness, the hooves of the horses rustled among the stubble, their thick shining necks bent to the ground as they searched for new grass. One morning he stood with his wife and the child, on the back porch, watching as a coyote followed his dog in from the field. Thin, vulnerable and alone, hunted for bounty on the open prairie, it paced on the last ridge, refusing to come any closer.

And each day the child grew. In the bathtub, secure between his legs, she splashed and screamed, while he sat behind, slowly washing her.

"Duck! Duck! Duck!" she yelled, over and over, while a wooden boat and yellow duck bobbed before her in the bathtub.

Fraser carefully wiped her back. The dark, wet curls almost reached to her neck, curving upward in a small, chaotic flurry of beauty. Her blue mark had almost disappeared, leaving her skin tanned and brown. Wet and slippery, still waving her arms and screaming for her duck, he handed her to his wife who waited with a towel. When she was dried for bed, Fraser sat with the child, looking at the book.

"Once upon a time there were some pirates. They sailed to a mountain."

Actually, they just drifted. Anyone could tell by looking at the pirates that they lacked the responsibility, the foresight, to sail anywhere, to consciously plan, chart, and carry out a predetermined voyage. Three of the pirates had very long hair, a fourth wore a bandana and earrings, and the fifth, short, bald, and with a black patch over one eye, affected a gaily coloured sash around his waist. The five pirates grinned crazily out of the book at the two of them. No. Sailing was definitely not their style. They drifted, floating with the tides, riding the winds, bumping into mountains, pillaging merchant vessels, fighting an army of dwarfs, kidnapping children. He turned the page. The child's tiny brown finger shot out, pressing into the round green stomach of a curious small creature.

"Dwar . . . ! Dwar . . . !" she began, each time her word trickling off into a series of excitedly jumbled syllables.

What kind of material were the identical jerkins the dwarfs wore made of he wondered. They were green, loden green, only not as muted, with a sheen to it, like moss that had been dried in the sun. He turned to their favourite page.

"One day the pirates found some children. The pirates kept the children for their wives to cook for them. The wives cooked nice things for the pirates. The pirates liked the fish best. They caught the fish themselves from the sea."

Five girls, beaming with the same expression as the pirates, carried exotic dishes to a table already brimming with delights. The pirates could not be seen. Presumably, they were still on deck, sunning themselves, and never entered the galley until supper was ready. Everyone seemed pleased with this arrangement.

He carried the sleeping child to her crib. Above her a mobile of fish swam from the ceiling, caught in a shaft of evening light from the west window.

One afternoon they went to the river. Piggyback, perched on his shoulders, she proclaimed from her height joyful exclamations in a language Fraser understood only by tone and sound, all the time pulling and tugging at his hair as if it were the reins of a horse. The prairie wind beat against them, bending the blades of new spring grass.

"Duck! Duck! Duck!" she screamed.

From a still, calm side-pool at the river's edge, the routed mallard, frightened by the child's excited shouts, pushed against the water. As it hurried through the full muddy pool, its neck thrust out in panic, a V-shaped wave rose from its breast, moving outward 'til it touched the shore. Wings thrashing and beating the water, it took flight, moving parallel with the water, so close its webbed feet trailed and skipped across the river's surface, until finally it rose above them. In every pool left by the melted snow, in every full ditch at the side of the road, they heard the chorus of returning ducks and geese. The sky was alive with them.

Upstream, visible in the distance only as a group of timbers clustered together, a raft drifted around the bend in the river. As it came nearer, he put down the child to gain a better look. Now Fraser could make out a man at the rear, separated from the others, guiding the raft with a long pole. They heard voices, a ragged attempt at singing lost in the rush of the river. He strained to catch the words of the song.

What *were* the words of the song?

There was so little time.

From the raft the strangely tinted glass of uplifted bottles glinted in the sun, mingling with the lyrics and the bright colours worn by the five men floating toward them.

On the shore, two children stood, waving, calling to them, waiting for the raft to land.

The Women on the Bridge

Battleford, November, 1884

AS THE GOWANLOCKS' BUCKBOARD APPROACHES THE BRIDGE BELOW Battleford, Indian women converge on the wagon and prevent their crossing.

Theresa Gowanlock's husband of two weeks talks to them in Cree. Twenty-eight-years-old and beginning to bald, John Gowanlock has a thin face and the harried look of a man seeking his fortune in the North-West. He explains they are on the last leg of a long journey, have no supplies left and nothing to give them. Theresa doesn't understand Cree, but sitting beside her husband on the buckboard and looking into the weathered brown faces of the women, she senses he is telling them this.

There are seven women and a dog pulling a small travois, poles crossed on its harnessed shoulders. They surround her with their foreign presence, their eyes touching each detail of her clothing, until finally, stripped naked, it is she who is foreign, one of the only white women in the Territory.

She cannot possibly know what the small bundles piled on the travois contain, only that whatever is within them may be the sum of their worldly possessions. Still, beneath the blankets they wrap themselves in, they are, like her, women. She wonders how they live, how they survive, and how they have come to be here on the bridge.

They must have been hidden by the poplar trees that line the far side of the riverbank. The Gowanlocks have arrived in late fall and ice is already forming at the river's edge. It breaks off in shards that swirl downriver. Beyond the bridge she sees a few squat buildings.

"Our welcoming committee," says her husband and flicks the reins. The horses jerk the buckboard into motion as the women quickly move aside. "Welcome to Battleford, my dear!" he shouts. "Formerly the capital of the North-West Territories." Is it irony, anger, or both, that she hears in his voice?

Her husband urges the horses forward as she turns to look back at the small ragged band of women who hold her vision even as they recede from it.

"I want you to wait in town until the house is finished," he tells her.

She cannot believe he would leave her in such a desolate God-forsaken place as Battleford. "Let me go with you," she begs.

"I want everything to be ready, the house perfect for you. Stay here with the Lauries. I'll go on to Frog Lake and send for you when the house is ready. It won't be more than a month. I promise."

Patrick Laurie's brother, Richard, is John Gowanlock's partner in the Frog Lake enterprise. Patrick Laurie is also the writer, editor, publisher, and printer of a one-man newspaper, *The Saskatchewan Herald*. Like everything else in Battleford, the *Herald* was founded on the premise that Battleford would remain the capital of the North-West and on the route of the proposed railway.

Laurie stands in frozen mud in the middle of nowhere in front of a ramshackle structure surrounded by a bastion of upright and askew fence posts he calls his editorial office. "What a little sheet!" he proclaims, proudly waving a page proof at her.

Humouring him, Theresa nods her head enthusiastically. Privately, she thinks him quite mad. Since she has been staying with the Lauries, she has learned a great deal about Laurie, and by reading his newspaper, a great deal about the region.

Patrick Gammie Laurie fancies himself an advance guard of settlement, sending word from the outer edge of the frontier back to a more civilized world. "That great Canadian journalistic pioneer," the *Hamilton Spectator* calls Laurie, who reprints this description of himself in the pages of his own paper.

When Theresa isn't helping Laurie's wife, Effie, with chores, she reads back issues of his newspaper, anxious to understand where she is. For the first time she learns of the four-day confrontation between the police and the combined war parties of Big Bear and Poundmaker that very summer. Why hasn't her husband told her about this? The newspaper is full of it. What is he hiding? Why has he gone ahead without her?

She discovers it then, the announcement of her wedding and as she reads it sees her marriage in an alarming new light.

MARRIED
GOWANLOCK – JOHNSON.

On Wednesday, October 1st, at the residence of the bride's father, by the Rev. Wardner, John A. Gowanlock, of Battleford, Saskatchewan Territory, to Miss Theresa M., daughter of Mr. H. Johnson, of Tintern, Lincoln Co., Ont.

J.A. Gowanlock, who went east some weeks ago to purchase machinery for a grist and saw mill to be put up at Frog Lake by himself and R.C. Laurie, returned on Friday last, and on his arrival here found the gratifying intelligence awaiting him that the machinery had arrived at Swift Current. It is intended to put in two run of stones, but for the present they will only bring one run and a forty-four inch saw. The building will be ready for the machinery by the time it arrives. Mr. Gowanlock has closed his store here and will go out to the lake next week. While down east he took unto himself one of Ontario's fair daughters and brought her out west to grow up with the country.

She scans the two paragraphs in the newspaper to see where the part about her marriage ends and the part about the mill machinery begins, but it is all one piece.

"Tacked on the end like some afterthought," she sighs, as the six-week stale news falls to her bed.

What a fool she'd been to allow this to happen to her. At first it had seemed so romantic, an adventure. Her betrothed, a young man from Parkdale, Ontario, had gone west seeking his fortune. Had he not strategically placed himself at what promised to be the gateway to the Territory, the hub of commercial activity and capital of the North-West Territories, Battleford? It seemed so. And at what point did she first realize that all was not as it seemed?

She does not confront these disturbing thoughts directly, but rather, obliquely. They nag at the corners of her mind and when they become too disquieting, too real, she dismisses them.

"A place for everything and everything in its place," her mother would say. She hates not having her own place. It heightens her disorientation, her sense of being alone in an unknown country. She tells herself she will feel better when her things arrive and she unpacks them. She longs to surround herself with familiar tangibles.

Six weeks he's left her waiting in Battleford while he's up at Frog Lake with thirteen men working on the dam, the mill, the house, left her waiting like a piece of machinery for his mill.

She wraps herself in a shawl, then realizes this will not be enough and puts on her coat. She shuts the door, and steps outside. A plain-looking woman, she wears her dark hair parted in the middle and tied in a bun. Against the advice of the Lauries, she has taken to walking about the town alone. In the intervening six weeks of waiting for her husband's return, fall has turned to winter and second thoughts about her marriage to serious misgivings.

She is walking in the new upper town just then being built and to which people are moving from the flats on the south side of the Battle River where it floods each spring. By relocating on higher land between the Battle and Saskatchewan Rivers, residents hope to escape the hazards of floods, and by being next to the Mounted Police barracks, the increasing resentment of the thousands of Crees that surround them.

As she makes her way beyond the single street and stands looking into the valley below, she feels utterly and completely alone, abandoned, like one of the empty shacks on the Battleford River flats: skinny logs that lie length-wise no higher than the reach of the man who put them there, a cotton sack for a window, a piece of rawhide hanging from a door frame.

"Men," her mother warned her, "when left to their own devices, most certainly run amok in the worst possible ways. But you'll see plenty of that where you're going. That's why they need us, to civilize them."

Now that the town is moving to higher ground it exists in two different places, but because of the split in opinion over the location of the townsite, fully and finally in neither, a town that can't make up its mind. Like some men. Like her husband.

Her eyes follow the cold green river coiling and uncoiling through the bare trees. She searches the valley below, wondering what is across the bridge, on the other side, the wilderness that claims her husband and from which he will soon return to take her to Frog Lake.

Though she does not see it at first, her mind filled with concern for herself and her husband, a stray horse stands on the bridge Theresa Gowanlock stares down upon from the height of the hill. The horse has caught a rear hoof between the timbers and is trapped, its fate already sealed. She sees it now. It paws the air in panic, then collapses in exhaustion. The mare lies on its side gathering strength, for surely, she recognizes this in its vulnerability, it is a mare.

From the far side of the river, three Indian women begin walking toward the bridge. As they approach it and begin to walk across, she is reassured that they will know what to do about the unfortunate horse now heaving on its side.

The three women bend over the horse and she glimpses the flash of their knives as they fall upon the mare.

With its scaffolding and plank deck, the bridge is like a wooden stage suspended above the bottom of the valley. She is held, fascinated, unable to avert her eyes from the scene unfolding below.

While the women work with their knives, the horse's legs thrash in short spasmodic twitches. One of the women folds the slippery hide while the other two carve the carcass into pieces they can carry. They hurl away the hooves and the head, and fling the intestines in an arc that ends with a splash in the water below. There are other women on the bridge now. They carry off a half-haunch and disappear through the trees. Others follow, carrying huge chunks of the horse. Theresa Gowanlock stares down on the butchering below, unable to believe it is happening, unable to stop watching.

In less than twenty minutes all evidence of the horse and the women is gone and it is possible to believe for just a moment that she did not see the slaughter, that it didn't happen. She has mistakenly opened the door to the wrong room and has seen something she shouldn't have seen. Now she tries to shut it. On the bridge between settlement and wilderness, she has glimpsed a part of the country she had not known existed, where the only law is the reality dictated by the moment. But the door in her mind will not stay shut. She does not think of them first as Indians or savages, but as women. She tries to imagine their circumstances, but she can't. She can't begin to.

And where were their men? She hadn't seen a single man. When she returns to the Laurie's house she asks Effie about them.

"If you mean that heathen bunch what whoop and beat the drum all day long in front of Sandy Macdonald's store disturbin' decent Christians with their infernal beggin' dance, they's gone back to Frog Lake and that's not near far enough away for me. Why can't they get themselves onto a reservation where they belong?"

Theresa Gowanlock hasn't been in the country long enough to develop such firm convictions about these matters, but she listens to the woman's loud bitterness with considerable alarm. "You mean to say," she asks, "they don't have a reservation?"

"This bunch never signed no treaty," replies the woman. "This used to be a decent place till the government got it into their heads we didn't need a railroad and Battleford wasn't the capital of the North-West anymore. And what do we get instead? Why we get the Indians. It's their fault. Them and that damn Dewdney!"

Since the disquieting scene on the bridge nothing seems certain. The capital is not the capital, the town is moving to a new site, Big Bear's band has not settled on a reserve. She is married but without her husband.

She believes that in essential matters of business the men know what they are doing. The mill at Frog Lake, the cutting of lumber, the dealings with the Indians, these things the men control and do well.

She clings to the belief that once she arrives at Frog Lake and surrounds herself with familiar objects in her own house, she will learn to feel at home in this alien land. She must, for it is all she has left. She envisions her new home as the place of her happiness, a foundation of stability in a wilderness of flux and change, and longs for her husband to come and take her there.

"I thought I'd go mad," she breathes. "Promise you'll never leave me like this again, John." Secure in his arms, her head against his chest, she does not tell him what she has seen and learned in his absence.

The next morning they load their wagon with supplies and begin their final journey to the distant outpost of Frog Lake. Tools, sacks of flour, and salted pork give the wagon a weight that carries it with gathering momentum into the bottom of the river valley where, before she can prepare for it, the bridge looms before her.

The actual clop-clop of the horses' hooves hit the timbers first, then the wagon itself. Now she sees it all again, not from the distance of the hill, but so close it is as if she is actually there with the women at the butchering, each detail magnified over and over in her mind: the arc of the animal's steaming guts flung from the bridge unfurl in the cold winter air over the river, tearing something loose within her until all she can do is scream and scream again as her husband stands in the buckboard, both arms reining the horses to a halt.

In the stillness of the stopped wagon and the warmth of his embrace, she closes her eyes and feels herself suspended somewhere between the life she left in Ontario and the place her husband is taking her. She opens them again and glimpses, between gaps in the planking, jagged chunks of ice on the cold swift current. And there, soaked into the boards by rain, beneath the thin clear sheet of ice forming on the planks, the blood of the horse.

"Please, let's not stop here," she says.

And her worried husband, helpless to understand any of this, can do nothing now but drive the horses on.

The wagon trundles across the bridge with a clatter, gains the other side, climbs the steep incline and disappears into the trees.

Dinner at Fort Pitt

Fort Pitt, December, 1884

"TO KEEP THE ANIMALS IN," John Gowanlock says as they walk through the unguarded front gate of the fence that surrounds the rough-hewn, spruce log structures inside.

He means livestock, she knows, staring up at the steep-pitched rooftops, thinking that since arriving in the North-West she has seen behaviour that certainly could lead her to believe otherwise, her gaze dropping to the snowbound yard where her growing disbelief in the difference between men and animals is further confirmed.

Four men examine a fur, pulling and tugging at the pelt.

"Red fox," enthuses her husband. "This is the season."

She feels the hard look of a lean, blond young man, barely twenty, who has already been places she hopes she will never go. Passing close to the crew of men who tug at the four points of the pelt, she avoids his eyes, first by looking down at the fur, each hair of the fox tipped with white and silver grey, then glancing up at the building her husband guides her toward.

It is the main building, the one most resembling a dwelling where people might live, though she can't imagine who. Small blank second-storey windows stare down at her trapped in her husband's world. Closer, she watches the black iron handle turn in the arched timber door and imagines the people on the other side: traders and unseemly adventurers who smell bad and act worse. But the door opens instead on a woman wiping her hands on an apron, stepping forward, embracing her.

"I'm Helen McLean! I've heard so much about you from John, but he's kept you hiding in Battleford forever and now . . . " the McLean woman steps back, touching her lightly on the shoulders and looking into her face, "and now, here you are at last! Welcome to Fort Pitt!"

"And yes," she thinks, "but where exactly is Fort Pitt, and where, exactly, am I?"

"Poor dear!" the McLean woman says. "You must be tired from your journey. The girls will show you to your room. Girls!" she calls into the hallway. "Come and meet our guest.

"A little rest before dinner and you'll be good as new! We've asked a few friends to join us, nothing formal. Just some people in the area I know you'll want to meet. Eliza! Kitty! Come take Mrs. Gowanlock to her room!"

One of the girls takes her arm and guides her up the narrow wooden stairway. "I'm Elizabeth." Ahead, a tall girl with dark braids bounds up the steps two at a time. "That's Katherine."

The girls place her bags on a rug spread over the wide planked floor of a second-storey room and stare as if she is a curiousity from another world. "We're so glad you've come," bursts Elizabeth, breaking the shy silence of the room. "You must tell us everything. About your trip. What it's like in the East."

They stand on either side of her, each beginning a statement the other finishes, sisters so close they seem two halves of one person. "Just everything!" repeats Katherine.

But before she can speak a single word, Elizabeth changes the subject and says, "Kitty and I planned the setting so we can sit on either side of you at the table. We put Duncan next to Inspector Dickens. You'll see. It's perfect!"

"Mother says you must rest before dinner so we'll have to wait till then," Katherine quickly adds.

"In the meantime," offers Elizabeth, pointing at something Katherine holds, "you may find this a pleasant surprise."

Katherine passes it to her: a puzzle. She turns the tapered, hollow, cone-shaped object in her hands; fragments and pieces of something loose tumble inside.

"Look through the hole in the tapered end," urges Katherine. "Go ahead, try it."

She presses the mahogany cone to her eye and squints through a peephole into a world of translucent coloured glass. "This is so beautiful," forgetting for a moment where she is.

Tiny pieces of coloured glass rearrange themselves and tumble into a pattern of perfectly symmetrical six-fold illumination; endlessly changing, never repeated, one small turn of the cone and the snowflakes of coloured glass fall irrevocably into a new pattern.

"It's a kaleidoscope. Father got it for us," says Katherine as the sisters back toward the door on tiptoe. "It's all the fashion in London. It's done with mirrors."

The McLean sisters slip through the door, then pull their heads around to peer in and say, "We're going to help mother get ready now. Try to sleep. We'll wake you in time."

She enters a long dining hall aglow in candlelight reflected off silver that illuminates the faces of dinner guests watching the self-conscious newcomer take her place. As William McLean guides her to the table she thinks this: last night I stayed at a half-breed's house and drank tea made in the same water the potatoes were boiled in; tonight I am being escorted to dinner on the arm of the factor of Fort Pitt — a perspective to focus on while trying not to be overwhelmed by the grand formality of the dinner setting and the dress of the guests.

"We've put you with the girls, Mrs. Gowanlock," her host says from behind, moving her chair. "I'll sit with your husband."

John is counting on her to make a good impression. It is essential to his business. A government contract to build a mill at Frog Lake. Trading with the Indians. Land and timber deals. The truth is she has been married two months to a man moving fast on the far edge of the frontier, a man who combined their honeymoon with a trip east to buy machinery and then left her waiting six weeks in Battleford.

But at last, here are the girls! How beautiful they look, changed now from the plain dark woolen house dresses of this afternoon to forest-green velvet and garnet satin. An unusual necklace made of thin cylinders of bone strung together with large brass beads moves against Katherine's dress.

How do they manage, cut off from the civilized world, to dress in the height of fashion from the pages of *The Young Ladies Journal* or *The Queen*? But their father is the factor of a Hudson's Bay post and she mustn't stare or let on that this Sunday dinner is different from any other Sunday of her life.

"Duncan will say grace," announces the father from the far end of the table.

"Dear Lord," intones Duncan.

A raised turquoise border encircles a painting by William Bartlett of the Chaudierè Bridge in the centre of the plate set before her bowed head. Duncan is still saying grace and no one will notice she hasn't closed her eyes. How peaceful the bridge is, so different from the one at Battleford where the Indian women . . . but she won't think of that, not now, cherishing instead the idyllic scene painted on her plate, and she cannot help herself, now while the others have their heads bowed, their eyes closed, she must, she will touch it. The tips of her fingers move over the raised floral pattern of the turquoise border as she drifts with two small sailboats painted on a mirrored surface of porcelain, and then the moment shatters, sudden and sure as if the plate itself has shattered in her hands — someone is watching her. But who? She is afraid to look up but knows she must. How embarrassing!

It is Elizabeth, her conspiratorial smile telling her the secret of the plate is safe. The sisters have been watching throughout grace, carrying on a silent conversation of grimaces, meaningful glances, and barely suppressed laughter.

These girls — a distraction and pure mischief. She must ignore them and concentrate instead on sinking her fork into a slice of lamb while her husband talks to McLean about the mill at Frog Lake and the house he has built.

"Of course, there's some inside finishing work still to be done."

She listens, intent for tangible details to help her envision the new home she will see for the first time two days' journey from tonight.

"You see," her husband speaks to the Hudson's Bay factor with an earnest intensity reserved for those he thinks important enough to advance his station in life, "a grand opportunity is opening to trade with the Indians up there. I want to put in some trade goods and a small store on the main floor of the house."

Two months' journeying to her home, and before she gets there, her husband has built a trading post in it. Worse, she learns of it second-hand, listening in on a conversation. He insists on keeping things from her, business matters she is not privy to and yet to which, as his wife, her fate is inextricably bound. He leads a life quite separate from her. She feels betrayed, cheated, alone.

"Aren't you rushing into things too quickly with this mill of yours?" asks McLean.

"That may be true," counters her husband, "though I doubt the government would put the building of the mill out for tender if they didn't see a future for the area."

"What's the point of building a flour mill up there when the Indians haven't even settled on a reserve, much less planted any wheat?" asks McLean.

"Ah," sighs the military man with the bright red beard who sits next to Katherine's brother Duncan, "the Indians."

He must be the Inspector Dickens the girls spoke of. He seems to be talking to himself, for no one is listening but her, unnoticed.

"Frankly, I would have preferred the Cape. I have always had a fondness for elephants. But here I am in Canada, part of a police force protecting the western aborigine from whiskey traders."

He seems to shuffle through fragments of his life as he puzzles over his plight, a process she herself has become familiar with of late; like composing letters that explain where you are but having no one to send them to.

"Hiring me to thwart whiskey traders was rather like setting the fox to guard the chicken house," he says, staring straight ahead. "What would father think, if he could see me now?" Then, as if to share some confidence with her, he leans across the table and she too leans forward, straining to hear him.

"Stuck in the Canadian mud!" He slumps forward in his chair and his head bobs into a sleeping nod as he withdraws into mutterings that to him alone make sense.

"There's government for you, Gowanlock," says McLean. "I'm afraid Inspector Dickens is the only government up here and he had one leg in the bag long before dinner began. I've made my views known, but as you can see he is often not with us. No, the government doesn't give a damn about us and that's precisely why I worry about you and your mill at Frog Lake."

"Surely you aren't suggesting — " begins her husband.

"This fall the tension was terrible. The government ordered Indian agents to cut down on rations, and even then, to issue them only to those on reservations. Big Bear hasn't complied and his people are starving. He often comes to the fort, searching for what he cannot find. He wants only a fair deal and can't get one, so instead, he wanders the countryside, an old man asking questions no one can answer. Reminds me a bit of Lear, don't you see?" McLean pauses, wiping the corner of his mouth with a napkin. "A dethroned monarch wandering the countryside. And like Lear, the offspring have turned on their father. And there are others. Wandering Spirit is being drawn into their circle. Little Poplar has come all the way from Montana to be a part of this."

"A part of what?" asks her husband.

"Aren't you forgetting something?" Helen McLean interrupts.

"I don't think so. I thought it a rather good analogy."

"Except for one important difference. Lear's daughters turned on him, but in the case of Big Bear it is his son." The McLean woman looks directly at her husband. "It is the men, not the women, who spoil things here, and quite frankly, I think you're spoiling our dinner! I'm sure our young bride from Ontario doesn't care to hear of such matters, having only just arrived. Do you, my dear?"

Everyone is waiting for her reply, but she can't think of what to say. She only knows she keeps hearing of Big Bear and his band of Plains Cree who have not settled on a reservation, and that her husband plans to trade with these same Indians out of their house. Her hand shakes so badly she sets her fork down on the tablecloth.

McLean balls a napkin in his closed hands.

A very old man with a brown weathered face and a snow-white beard bends over the table and places a dish on it. In the silence he seems to take forever.

McLean's crumpled napkin falls to the table. "I'm afraid you've outdone yourself tonight," he tells the old man in a cheerful tone, as if the ominous discussion had never taken place.

The old man must be the cook and at last she sees her opening. "Yes," she says in a pleasant, almost trance-like voice, "the lamb is quite lovely."

One of Katherine and Elizabeth's younger sisters rolls her eyes in amusement. "It's not lamb, it's beaver!

Kitty, why don't you tell Mrs. Gowanlock about our Indians."

"Yes, do," urges Duncan. "You must, you know."

"Sitting Bull traded six ponies for these beads and gave them to me before he left the country." Katherine holds them out from her dress for her to see. "It's because I'm such a good shot. Besides, I was his favourite."

If she were their age she too might see this as an adventure, instead of feeling fear for herself and her husband.

"Really girls!" Helen McLean rushes from the kitchen to scold her daughters. "What will our guest think if you carry on this way? Please, take Mrs. Gowanlock to the parlour where we can rest and leave these men to themselves.

"I know how you must feel," she says, "coming here like this in the dead of winter. But wait until spring when you can listen to the wind in the poplars and watch it comb through the grass. I have lived in this country all my life and, like my husband, my father was a Hudson's Bay factor. There is so much I want to show you. Look at these girls. They love their life here. Born and raised in the country, like their mother."

"It was a lovely dinner," Theresa says.

"Our cook, Otto Dufresne, deserves the credit. He knows the country so well. How to get the most of it. That's the key out here. To adapt."

"You seem to have adapted very well," she hears herself say.

Within the walls of the fort the McLeans have created their own inner world of family. Can she too dare to dream of having her own children, of raising a family in this wilderness?

"Come and see," says Helen McLean. "We have the only organ in the West just waiting in the parlour to be played."

"Do you know 'The Lost Chord'?" asks Elizabeth.

"It's our favourite," says Katherine. "You must join us."

The girls gather around their mother and Duncan follows his sisters, leaving only her husband, McLean, and the military man, Inspector Dickens, now unsuccessfully attempting to rise from the dinner table.

"I have already had the pleasure of hearing 'The Lost Chord' sung by the McLeans." He grasps the back of his chair for support. "Believe me when I say, Mrs. Gowanlock, once you have heard their unique rendition, the word lost will take on new meaning." He lurches from his chair and weaves down the hallway.

"I'm afraid it's our Inspector who is lost," Duncan says. "But never mind all that, Mother's setting up in the parlour."

Ranging in age from Elizabeth and Katherine to the small girl in the chocolate brown dress who peers at her through bangs, the McLean children sit in the parlour in a circle around their mother, waiting for her to join them.

"I only play it when we have company," Helen McLean says, seated at her great pride.

Ignoring their mother, the McLean children attempt to outdo each other telling tales of their experiences with the Indians. Duncan claims to have been adopted by a band of Saulteaux at birth, while Kitty says Sitting Bull made her an Indian princess.

"Have you met Charles Dickens's son?" asks Duncan, realizing he can't top his sister with Indian stories.

"Of course not," she replies. The abruptness of her answer reflects the impatience of a full day spent travelling across the country, the dinner, unravelling now into a nonsensical riddle. Confused, she wonders aloud, "How could I?"

"He lives right here in the fort," Duncan says. "I thought I saw him talking to you at the table, but perhaps he was talking to himself. He often does, you know."

"Lives here in the fort?" she hears herself say, and at this precise moment senses something happening to her. She is becoming one of the children, for they have drawn her into their circle. "Lives in the fort?" she repeats. "Who lives in the fort?"

"In the barracks," Duncan says. "Next time you're here, we'll visit. Inspector Dickens is in charge of our Mounted Police. Imagine. Our defence, if it should ever come to that, but of course, it won't, would be in the hands of the son of a famous novelist. Wouldn't that be an adventure?"

"Yes. Imagine," she says. "Imagine that!" But she cannot and will not imagine such a thing.

Hands poised, their mother looks down from the organ, signals she is ready. With a nod to the girls, she strikes the keys, and over the rich sonorous sound of the organ float the words to "The Lost Chord".

> *It quieted pain and sorrow,*
> *Like love overcoming strife.*
> *It seemed the harmonious echo*
> *From our discordant life.*
> *It linked all perplexed meanings*
> *Into one perfect piece,*
> *And trembled away into silence*
> *As if it were loath to cease.*

In the circle of children she no longer feels alone. The music is having a quite different effect on her than that predicted by the bitter lonely man who spoke to her at the dinner table. Inspector Dickens. Imagine. Charles Dickens's son.

She sits on the floor holding hands with Katherine and Elizabeth and for the first time in months feels outside herself and her fears as, swept up in the song and the power of the organ, she joins in the singing:

> *I have sought, but I seek in vain,*
> *That one lost chord divine,*
> *Which came from the soul of the organ*
> *And entered into mine.*

Something is wrong; not the song, not the melody, but the words. Without warning, in mid-verse, the girls have abruptly switched to Cree and she is no longer able to sing with them.

Is this what Inspector Dickens meant by a unique rendition that would give new meaning to the word lost? If so, then it is the cruelest of jokes, for though the Cree sung by the McLean girls has a pleasant enough musical quality it is completely foreign to her and quite suddenly it is she who is lost.

She is not part of the McLeans or the life they lead at Fort Pitt and never can be. Separate and shut off from the real world, clothed in the latest fashion, waited on by servants, Helen McLean and her children live an extravagant illusion. The walls of Fort Pitt are blinders behind which the McLeans maintain a myopic denial of who and where they are: a handful of whites in an unknown land surrounded by thousands of starving Indians.

The song in Cree cannot include her. An immense tiredness is enveloping and overwhelming her. The room turns like the girls' kaleidoscope, Katherine's and Elizabeth's upraised alarmed faces swirling into a blur as she falls into darkness.

She sits up in bed. What hour is it? Where is her husband? She doesn't know, only that it is night. She stares into the darkness of a room filled with fragments of a dream so frightening it has just wakened her: a horse trapped on the Battleford bridge . . . Indian women falling on it with their knives. In her dream she is on the bridge with the Indian women; in her dream she has become one of them. She is living the life of a Cree woman scavenging meat from a crippled horse caught on the bridge. How different from the elaborate meal served within the walls of Fort Pitt.

She parts the curtain: a flat expanse of snow illuminated by moonlight, and beyond the far edge of the field, the river that runs through her dream and churns under the bridge at Battleford, the North Saskatchewan.

Something terrible will happen. She feels a powerful foreboding, certain and irreversible as the river itself, its winding looping coils defined by the dark hills rising behind it.

Footsteps on the stairs. Someone is coming. She draws the curtain. In the darkened room, her husband, a man she doesn't know, steps quietly toward the bed believing she is asleep.

Skating on Thin Ice

Frog Lake, March 28, 1885

CAMERON LOCKED THE DOOR BEHIND HIM and looked into the grey northern sky — just enough light to get to Gowanlock's before nightfall if he skated instead of walking.

Striding toward the lake, he thought of the woman who passed him briefly in the yard at Fort Pitt, a pretty thing dragged along on the arm of her strong-willed husband. That was in December. Now it was the end of March, the ice was melting, and they had invited him for dinner.

Cameron walked toward the lake, his casual gait belying any fear he might feel as one of a small group of whites surrounded by Crees in this isolated settlement. As a trader, he knew that to gain their respect and friendship he must never show he was afraid. He wasn't always successful.

Cameron knelt at the lake's edge and looked into the film of water on the thawing ice at his reflection: the thin angular face of a young man who had survived a winter living alone in the wilderness. He bent to study it further and saw, mirrored in the reflection of the poplars, the barely discernible movement of a rider through the trees.

He did not turn to acknowledge the rider, seen only by chance, but instead trailed his fingers through the film of water, at once touching and dispelling the reflection. The Indians were everywhere a presence, and like the land, a mirror in which each man might find himself.

Even though he had no idea of ice conditions two miles down the creek where the young couple were building their mill, Cameron decided the ice on the lake would hold and resolved to skate to Gowanlock's for dinner. He sat on a log and strapped the blades to his boots. Then Cameron hobbled onto the wet ice and with a downward thrust of an angled blade glided in a wide arcing turn toward the south end of the lake. Searching the shore he no longer saw the Indian, but sighting the break in the trees that marked the mouth of the creek, he began skating toward it. In the rhythmic steady nicking slash of his skate blades, his thoughts streamed through the rush of the coming night as he remembered how he first came here.

. . . just a kid then and believing every word when cousin Joe Woods gave him a fire-bag he said belonged to a Sioux named Rain-in-the-Face when Joe was stationed with the Mounted Police at Fort Walsh.

"The coals of hell are in that fire-bag, and son, you play with fire, you'll get burned!" Not his father, long dead from a logging accident, but his grandfather, Bleasdell, warning him the day he almost burned the house down when he finally got the spark from the flint to catch.

Magic it was, filled with the wild smell of smoke-tanned leather and places he wanted to go. Suddenly his grandfather's stone vicarage and the shade trees that lined the streets of Trenton seemed tame and civilized.

He would go further west than his cousin, thousands of miles beyond Fort Walsh, where the western edge of the plains unroll into foothills, and lodge-pole pine and spruce climb the ragged looming wall of the Rockies. In the mountains, working on the railway until the summer of '84, he earned a stake for a trading outfit at Pincher Creek: eleven horses, blankets, traps, ammunition, bacon, tea, cloth, mirrors women can see themselves in, Perry Davis Pain Killer for the men.

"The frontier," cousin Joe told him, handing him the fire-bag. "So many buffalo, you can't imagine."

But the buffalo were just bones. No matter where he went, the best part of the country had vanished before he got to it — elusive, unreachable, always moving just ahead of him, a place in his heart he would never arrive at. The frontier.

Battleford had become too white and everyone in the south was waiting for the railway to freight them the same civilization he was trying to escape. So he headed north until he reached the last of the free Indians, a band of renegade Cree without treaty or reservation, wintering on the shore of the lake on which he now skated.

He didn't find his uncle's frontier, but he had certainly found the Indians. Surely it was more than coincidence, his being here. Some destiny or design had drawn him to them. Like himself they too were searching for their freedom, refusing to take treaty.

After he and Poundmaker's son broke trail south of Battleford through the Eagle Hills and on to Swift Current, the Cree called him Little Brother. He was twenty-two-years-old and some shared kinship of spirit prompted them to call him Little Brother . . .

His thoughts drifted in a free and unconscious reverie as he glided over the ice. He would never go back. Not like his cousin Joe, returning to Ontario. Until the day he died he would move always on the edge of things, an outsider, like these Indians.

The lone figure left the lake, moved into the narrowing mouth of the creek, and vanished among the trees. In the last lingering light of March 28, 1885, William Bleasdell Cameron skated slowly and carefully onto the six-foot wide ribbon of ice that wound through the poplars, birch, and spruce, colder now, and darker, on the creek.

Unlike the freedom of the open lake where he hadn't noticed the ice water thrown up by his skate blades splattering his thick wool pants to the knees, here, in the close confines of the creek, he felt the heavy weight of the water freezing in the falling temperature. The shock of frozen wool on his legs shuddered through him. Cameron stopped on the creek ice in the fading light and chill air and considered his folly. A log laden with snow slanted across the creek, blocking his way. He could easily climb over but *then* what? An unexpected combining of circumstances — a sudden drop in temperature, melting ice refreezing — and he was completely at the mercy of the elements.

He would never make it to Gowanlock's now. He had to get off the ice and keep moving toward the shelter and warmth of Big Bear's camp. He pulled his flannel-lined mitts off and unstrapped the blades from his boots, though not quickly enough, for when he replaced his mitts, his thumbs were numb. His boots crunched through the ice-glazed crust of snow that bordered the creek as he searched for the trail. Already he was losing feeling in his feet as he moved along the compacted snow of the trail that led back to the settlement through Big Bear's camp.

Finally, the smoke and smell of the Indian camp. Cameron staggered forward into startled Cree voices and snapping dogs and moved between tipis toward the main lodge. He dropped to his knees, lifted the lodge flap, and quickly crawled through the oval opening into the darkness inside.

Surprised, the men shifted their places in the circle to make room for him. Cameron gratefully placed his hands, palms out, toward the small fire. Warmth from the burning embers seeped into his body and as the cold dissipated in subsiding waves of pain, he glanced around the dark, smoke-filled tipi for faces familiar from trading at the Hudson's Bay store, the unmistakable and curiously wavy black hair of Wandering Spirit, and the broad defiant face of Big Bear's son, Imasees. But the others were not from Big Bear's tribe, nor was Big Bear himself here, he realized, becoming aware of the silence since he entered the tipi. He was overcome with an awkward sense that he had interrupted something.

The Indians stared into the fire, their dark faces tense, absorbed, and though the silence lasted only a moment, to Cameron it seemed to hang forever in the closeness of the tipi.

The men passed the stone pipe and began to speak in a guarded Cree completely different from the Pidgin-Cree they spoke for Cameron's benefit in the Hudson's Bay store. Ignoring him, they talked among themselves, excluding Cameron as completely as if he didn't exist. He was not connected to them, felt completely alone, and knew now he had interrupted a meeting at which he was not welcome, his presence scarcely acknowledged. Even though his clothes were not yet dry, Cameron's pride told him to leave.

He had thought he knew them, but he only knew that part which they had chosen to reveal, allowing him to think he was on familiar terms for their benefit, a façade of friendly banter across the counter of the Bay store for the young clerk when they wanted something. He had assumed he was in control, but it was they who were in control. Cold, calculating, they could manipulate him or turn on him as suddenly as the weather.

The rush of spring air that had swept him onto the ice had vanished in the raw north wind that whipped at the leafless limbs of the poplars.

"I am not lost," he told himself, his voice barely audible in the wind.

Light from a low rising quarter-moon reflected off the glazed snow crust and cast the poplars ahead in black silhouettes. Icy branches cracked in the wind and seemed to palpably scrape the cold air.

He thrust his mittened hands out to shield his eyes and face from the flicking lash of branches as he lunged through the forest, the meaning of his unexpected reception in the Indian camp turning over and over in his mind. He had been searching for the romance of an adolescent adventure. It was the myth of the West that had lured him, not its harsh reality. He was a romantic who had never known where he was until tonight.

As he pushed aside branches, a twig caught between the thumb and body of his mitten broke off and was held in his mittened hand. Half mad with cold, clutching the tiny branch which he waved in the air like some magic wand, William Bleasdell Cameron stumbled out of the trees and into the clearing at the Hudson's Bay store at Frog Lake.

Holy Thursday

Frog Lake, April 2, 1885

"WHAT TIME IS IT?"

Theresa Gowanlock is calling from the top of the stairs to a woman who shares her first name, Theresa, Theresa Delaney — an incredible coincidence considering they are the only two white women in the settlement.

"About 4:30," says the Delaney woman. "Judging by the light."

The two women stand in Theresa Delaney's kitchen in the first grey light before the dawn of Thursday, April 2, 1885.

"I hope I'm not disturbing you," apologizes Theresa Gowanlock. "But with all the guns going off and the dancing, I couldn't sleep. And just now I heard voices."

"Imasees and John Pritchard came to tell my husband the Métis have stolen our horses."

The night before last Pritchard had delivered a letter to Theresa Gowanlock and her husband from Agent Quinn advising them that the Métis had defeated Crozier at Duck Lake, and that they should leave their house at the mill and come to the settlement at once. Odd, she thinks, and says, "I wonder about that half-breed interpreter, John Pritchard. He knocks on our door with a letter from Quinn and then he comes to your house carrying messages from Big Bear's son. Who does he work for?"

"Why he works for himself," Theresa Delaney says, "like any interpreter. He may be the only man in the settlement who knows what's going on.

"Still, I don't think we really have anything to worry about. Our Indians have no grievances and no complaints to make," she insists. "They are happy in their home in the wilderness and I consider it a great shame for evil-minded people to instill into their excitable heads the false idea that they are persecuted by the government.

"When I say our Indians, I mean those under my husband's control. I look upon the Indian children as my children and my husband looks upon the men as being under his care. They regard him as their father." She pauses, watching her houseguest take in her words.

Theresa Gowanlock turns over in her mind the phrase first used by the McLeans, now by this woman: "Our Indians."

A staccato of rapid rifle fire scatters her thoughts, a sound she will never get used to, the random unfocussed violence of these sudden bursts of gunfire. A tense expectation fills the air. She hears it in the talk of the men and the demented out-of-control gunfire. She says, "And isn't there the slightest shadow of a doubt in your mind that not the Métis, but the Indians themselves might have taken our horses?"

"Always. Always, my dear. But even if it were true, it would never do to let them think, for even a moment, that we doubt their word.

"It's not that I'm braver than you," continues the Delaney woman. "I'm not. I just won't let them see. Once they see you are afraid, they take advantage. They come in here, right into my own kitchen and sit down and help themselves as if you'd made it all just for them. They are the worst possible freebooters."

There is a soft knock on the back door, barely discernible, as if someone knew that people were downstairs in the kitchen to answer it at this early hour. Theresa Delaney stands in the open doorway while a man talks to her in Cree, but Theresa Gowanlock's view of him is blocked by the Delaney woman's back. She watches the Delaney woman close the door, admiring her confidence but unsure of her judgement.

"That was Big Bear's son," says Theresa Delaney. "He feels sorry the horses have been taken. He and his men are entirely to blame. They danced all night and then fell asleep and it was then that the Métis took the horses. But we shouldn't worry because he, Imasees, King Bird, will personally start looking for the horses as soon as it is light." She says this in a rote monotone, remembering the words, translating them now for the Gowanlock woman.

King Bird. What a beautiful but odd and incongruous name for someone as implacable and stolid as Big Bear's son. No wonder most people call him by his Cree name, Imasees. "And do you believe him? What did you say?"

"Of course, I believe him. I told him it's almost light so he'd best get on with it."

But Theresa Gowanlock is not so easily reassured. Since she and her husband left their home at the mill and came to the settlement two days ago, the men have been in a continuous small informal meeting and whenever she gets within hearing they quickly change the subject, lapse into amenities about the weather, or worse, into silence; her husband huddled with the others in this, the latest phase of his betrayal. It is a bad sign, she thinks, when men and women do not share confidences. Already Quinn, Delaney, and her husband are discussing the stolen horses.

The Delaney woman leans across the table and in a low confidential voice says, "I have my own private opinions upon the causes of this latest unrest but do not deem it well or proper to express them. There are others besides the half-breeds and Big Bear and his men connected with this affair. There are many objects to be gained by such means and there is a wheel within a wheel in the North-West troubles.

"But never mind all that. Your hands are shaking! We'll take a brandy with our tea. It's the least we can do while we wait for this disturbance to end."

The Delaney woman stands on a chair and reaches onto a high shelf for a brandy bottle.

"That's a beautiful cupboard."

"Why thank you. Williscraft, the old man working at your husband's mill, made it for me. He has such a way with wood."

"Yes," Theresa Gowanlock hears herself say.

But of course, she knew that, recognized his work, for she has one very similar in her own kitchen, and admiring Theresa Delaney's only makes her realize how much she misses her new home and causes her quite suddenly to confront a terrible truth: she will never see it again, nor the treasured pieces of herself with which she so carefully filled it: the furniture from her mother and father's farm in Ontario, the china and family heirlooms that define who she is. Now there is no past and she has no identity; now there is only the tenuous present of a few articles of clothing she carries on her back.

"It will end, you know," Theresa Delaney is saying. "It always does. It's nothing really. You should have been here last summer. All of Battleford barricaded inside the fort for a week while the Indians faced off against the police and not a thing came of it, except in the end one of them went to jail. This is the same sort of thing. You'll see. Say when."

The Delaney woman pours brandy into Theresa Gowanlock's teacup and waits for her to say "when," but she is thinking of her house and doesn't, so finally the Delaney woman takes a small portion for herself, then stands on the chair to return the bottle to the cupboard. "Best not to leave the bottle on the table," she says. "Or for that matter, anything else you might want for yourself."

"My own house would be nice," says Theresa Gowanlock, standing, when the first wave of brandy hits her. She clutches the corner of the table as if it were the only tangible thing left in the world to hang onto.

"We're not like you," she insists, hovering over the Delaney woman who sits silent and amazed. "They are not our Indians. We, that is, my husband and I, do not work for the Department of Indian Affairs and we are not tied to these people in any way. No, we came out here on a business venture. How I ever let that man make me believe for even one minute that this was the land of opportunity I will never know.

"Battleford! That's all he could talk of. Battleford was supposed to be the capital of the North-West. Battleford was on the railway line. Then, overnight they change the route, Regina's the capital, and Battleford? Instead of the railroad, Battleford gets your Indians."

She feels better now that she has vented some of the tension but bad that the Delaney woman has borne the brunt of it. "I have no right. Not after the kindness you've shown me. I'm sorry."

"Don't be sorry, Theresa. There is no need. Not between you and me. Since you came in December I've begun to feel at home here for the first time. My life is no longer a lonely life. Now, more than ever, there are just the two of us. Don't think for a moment these men have the slightest control over things here, because they don't. They as much as admitted so yesterday."

Theresa Gowanlock thinks about her husband's error in judgement in predicting the economics of Battleford and their future. She thinks about her husband and the other men meeting in the Delaney house for two days, grappling with the reality of where they really are. And young Bill Cameron, just back from Big Bear's camp, claims the Indians behave as if they'd never known him; even Quinn, an old hand with the Sioux from the States who works for the Department here, said, "I know these Indians well enough to insist we should all leave the settlement immediately."

Inspector Dickens and his men have already left.

"You are on your own now, I'm afraid." Dickens attempted to impart this with some sobriety as the official notice of the departure of the police, but Theresa Gowanlock detected the demented glee in his announcement, as if for him, things were never right unless they had gone as horribly and irrevocably wrong as his own life. "Keep to your dwellings! It's not safe to be abroad!"

And if this is so, why, against the advice of both Quinn and Dickens, have her husband and the others decided to stay on? Stubborn pride. The need to assert that all is well and that the men are in control, when in fact even she can see that neither is true.

The horses have been stolen. Not that it matters; where would they go with horses? Yet without them their isolation is final, complete; they are cut off from the rest of the world. Big Bear's son has been looking for them. Just thirty minutes have elapsed since he reassured the Delaney woman he would find them and surely he has, for now he has returned.

From her chair where she sits at the kitchen table, she can see Imasees standing at the foot of the stairs looking up at them with his arms crossed, as if waiting for someone or something to descend. Half-way up stand Quinn and Delaney and further up, the fringed leggings of an Indian at the top of the stairs. And then without warning or notice she is suddenly watching, one by one, the wooden stock and blue metal of a Winchester rifle, three revolvers, another rifle, not a Winchester, but her husband's old single-shot Snider, the guns passing down from man to man to Imasees who stands at the bottom of the stairs collecting them.

"Exactly what is going on here?" Theresa Delaney asks her husband.

"Imasees and his men are short of firearms and they need ours to defend us from the Métis."

"For God's sake, man," interrupts Quinn, "let's drop the pretence, at least among ourselves. This thing could turn to soup fast. We are prisoners. They have our guns and they have our horses."

Outside somewhere a door is being smashed in — Dill's store or the police barracks. The looting has begun. She wonders what will be left of her house at the mill. They have given themselves over freely and in good faith to the Indians. They are no longer in control of their own lives. And not once did anyone ask her opinion. At what moment did the men decide, against the advice of the police, of Quinn, against all good sense, to stay on in the settlement?

Perhaps it was Father Fafard arguing that they should stay as a demonstration of faith. Or Theresa Delaney's husband thinking it would be a shame to abandon the government provisions. Hadn't Big Bear given John Delaney a peace pipe and told him he was beloved by all the band?

And at what point did the men realize the truth and decide to keep it from her? It doesn't matter now.

Outside, as each hammer blow of the axe smashes into the splintered door of Dill's store, something inside her is breaking: trust, suspension of disbelief, the veneer of her gullibility, wanting to believe Imasees and his men are protecting them from the Métis, all her hopes and aspirations, shattering one by one, blow by blow. She is on her knees now, stripped of all self-deception, naked in the knowledge she can no longer shut out, quietly crying to herself.

Absorbed in their own talk, the men are silenced by her soft sobbing, the sight of her huddled form cradled in the arms of Theresa Delaney.

She tries to stifle her crying and focus on faces blurred by tears: Big Bear, an anxious worried old man stripped of all power and control over his men; the broad implacable face of his son, Imasees; Wandering Spirit, Little Poplar. They are all here, some twenty Indians watching her, the white woman, the first to break.

One of them leans over to talk to her husband. Now her husband is trying to calm her, but she won't listen. He is saying, "They want you to know that you should not be afraid. They will not harm you."

But it is all lies. The men have already resumed talking. Her husband will deal with her now. Except she won't let him. She is being difficult. There, he says it, this man holding her by the wrists, shaking her, her husband, "Don't be difficult, Theresa."

She doesn't care. She will not be deceived any longer, not by him, not by any of them.

But she must regain control of herself or she will never know what is happening. If she just sits here quietly and watches, she can see Wandering Spirit talking to Quinn, demanding something. Big Bear's war chief shakes his fist at Quinn, poor Quinn, who tried to warn them. Now it is all coming down on him. She listens, trying to make out the words.

"Who is the head of the whites in this country?" Wandering Spirit demands. "Is it the government, or the Hudson's Bay Company, or who?"

Quinn can only answer with a harsh forced laugh. How little they know of us, she thinks, suddenly realizing the significance of Wandering Spirit's question and of Quinn's bitter laugh.

The toll of the church bell echoes through the small settlement and across Frog Lake — Holy Thursday. This morning it will be John Pritchard's boy, his hands wrapped around the rope, ringing in early morning mass. The day, she realizes, as the church bell clashes with the yells of the Crees pillaging Dill's store, has hardly begun and anything might happen.

"I think you should all go to church and pray," says Wandering Spirit. "But first," he adds as an afterthought, "my men will kill an ox."

"Why yes!" John Delaney jumps up. "That can be arranged."

But Wandering Spirit is merely informing him what his men intend to do, not asking his permission. Delaney no longer has any power or control here. Does anyone, she wonders. It comes to her now why Wandering Spirit's question to Quinn disturbs her. The Indians do not have a plan. They are making this up as they go along, and for her, this is even more frightening.

"Go to the church," Wandering Spirit demands, moving through the house.

"We'd better go with the others," her husband says, as if they have any choice in the matter.

She tightly grasps her husband's hand and begins walking slowly up the hill toward the church, the Delaneys, Quinn, the other whites, and the Indians behind them.

The smell of burning wood fills the air. Dill's store is in flames and the Indians dart in and out of the smoke and move hurriedly between buildings. Amidst the smoke and raucous cries, the steady, strangely out-of-place ringing of the church bell, she moves up the hill, as in a trance.

Wandering Spirit circles the group on horseback and just as they reach the top of the hill catches sight of Cameron. "Why don't you go to church with your friends?" he shouts, waving his arm toward the others.

She wonders what will happen if Cameron decides to disobey this thinly veiled order, but the young Hudson's Bay clerk quickly joins the procession.

Theresa Gowanlock and her husband move between two armed Indians standing guard on either side of the church door. As they step inside, young Father Marchand, down from Onion Lake to assist in the service, is about to close the door but is stopped by

Father Fafard. "Let the doors remain open so those who wish may enter."

Fafard turns and walks down the aisle, toward the altar, his back to the congregation, so that she and everyone else in the church except Fafard himself see Wandering Spirit's silent moccasined feet stalk down the aisle behind the priest who, stooping forward now to don his white vestments, steps to the altar and turns to see, here, in the centre of his church, the upturned face of Wandering Spirit, his face streaked with black war paint, his Winchester butt-ended and pointing heavenward, Wandering Spirit kneeling before him, his rifle in his hand.

The small church seethes with the energies of these two men, this conflict between a priest and his congregation of Woods Cree on one side, and on the other, a war chief and his Plains Cree warriors. Standing at the back of the church Theresa Gowanlock hovers on the periphery, on the brink of this clash of opposites that threatens to consume them all.

And at the centre, Father Fafard begins the invocation in Cree, then falters, as the Plains Cree outside whoop and holler and move through the open door strutting and weaving into the church.

"I forbid you to do any harm," Father Fafard tells them. "Go away quietly to your camps and do not disturb the happiness and peace of the community."

Wandering Spirit rises and faces his own men. "Go!" he shouts.

As the Plains Cree shuffle out of the church, they glance back at their leader who waves his rifle at the whites huddled in the rear of the church. "Go to his place," he says, his rifle pointing at John Delaney.

When Theresa Gowanlock and the others come out of the church they are surrounded by armed Indians waiting to escort them back to the Delaneys'. They are almost fifty feet down the hillside when Little Bear, glancing back from his horse, sees Father Fafard silhouetted against the church door, about to close it. He wheels his horse and gallops back to the church. The priest has almost closed the door when Little Bear leaps from his horse, forces the door open and pumps his fist into Father Fafard's eye.

"Hurry and catch up with the others," orders Little Bear.

Hands pressed to his face, the priest staggers forward, a small robed figure stumbling blindly down the hill toward her. This is the end, Theresa Gowanlock thinks, the end of everything.

The Delaney house has become a central gathering place to which the Indians are directing all the whites in the settlement, for what purpose and to what end she dares not imagine.

Wandering Spirit keeps trying to get information from Quinn. Who is their leader? The Queen? The government? The Hudson's Bay? Who is it? It strikes her again how little knowledge these people have of the world she comes from.

Cameron is ordered to the Bay store to provide the Indians with whatever they request. Father Fafard's eye is already swollen shut. Chief, in name only, Big Bear alternately offers reassurance and warning.

"I am afraid," he blurts to John Delaney, "afraid some of my young men will shoot the whites." Then quickly adds, "But don't worry. You will be safe."

No one is in control. Wandering Spirit gives orders, but Imasees is always present. Silent, since the deception of the horses.

For surely it was deception. She senses his hand in things, though in what way she cannot tell.

Perhaps it is the continued pretence that these Cree warriors are protecting them from the half-breeds, an extension of the story of the stolen horses with which Imasees began the morning, that makes her think this. Imasees, standing at the bottom of the stairs collecting the guns. Their guns.

Wandering Spirit wants everyone to go to the Indian camp, but Quinn is arguing with him.

"We will all go to our camp now, so that we can be together and defend you better from the half-breeds."

This is all a lie. But to what end, she wonders.

Quite unexpectedly her husband comes to her. "You had best put your shawl around you for it is very cold," he says, as if they are going for a walk together, but then adds, "Perhaps we will not be gone long."

But he doesn't really know and what he says makes very little sense, though now that she thinks about it, no more and no less than anything else he has ever said.

She has been walking for some time now, her back to the ruin of black smoke billowing from the church and the gunfire in the distance behind her. She is no longer startled by the shots as when they woke her this morning, for there has been intermittent gunfire ever since. This just serves to illustrate, she thinks, listening to the latest burst of shots from somewhere behind her, how you adapt to circumstances, even when the circumstances are out of control.

The trail to the Indian camp breaks out of the poplars into a field that hints of spring in the sight ahead: George Dill and his dog, running alongside each other, a small spaniel jumping playfully at his master's leg. Dill thrusts his head back and pumps his arms wildly, running full out now, the dog bounding and snapping excitedly at his leg, the dog believing this all a game, and perhaps it is, for all around Dill lead zips and thunks softly into the spongy wet spring ground and he is almost there, almost to the cover of the bushes beyond the edge of the field when a bullet spins him around and sends him toppling backward into the poplars.

Two men run past her.

"Don't shoot!" one of them screams as his hat flies from his head and she sees by the shock of his white hair that it is Charles Williscraft, the old carpenter, helpless and bareheaded, running for his life, "Oh, don't shoot!"

She turns in the direction of the firing to see a rider aim down on her husband.

"I am shot," he says, and staggers away from her, then turns and stumbles back, clutching his chest with both hands.

His legs crumple as she catches him under his arms, his weight pulling her down.

"I am so sorry," he says.

"Hold still," she soothes, cradling him in her arms.

Slumping forward, his chin on his chest, he watches her unbutton his blood-soaked shirt to a chest wound percolating air and blood, and it is the last thing he sees, his life slipping away, so warm, as it seeps across the back of her hand touching the wound, the small splintered fragments of bone between her fingers.

Leaning over him, she sets his head on the ground and, unable to look at his eyes, glances up for the first time since the shooting and sees no one standing in the field. No one. Just the dog at the edge of the field, tail wagging, head poked into the bushes where Dill fell. If she gets up she too will surely be shot. She is afraid to move. There is nothing she can do but lie here beside a dead man and let the cold ground seep into her.

The dog whimpers and sniffs at Dill's body and lets out a long low whine that builds to a howl, then turns and lopes across the field to discover the others. Each time it finds a body, it turns in a frenzy on its hind legs, yelping incessantly.

She flinches as a Cree wheels on his horse, takes aim, and with a single shot silences the dog. Clenched tightly against the body of her dead husband, she watches through squinted, almost-closed eyes as the riders move toward her. Crisscrossing the field they weave in and out among the corpses, so close the hooves shake the ground.

A rider reins in, his horse hovering right over her. Its nostrils nuzzle under her arm, its breath brushes down her back. She must lie perfectly still, but can't, soaked through to her skin, trembling so with fear and cold. At the first touch of hands on her back she scrambles to her feet, moving away in terror from an astonished Cree who stands and stares after her.

She trips and stumbles over Father Marchand's leg. A young Indian boy tears dead grass from the ground and, wadding it into a ball, daubs at the gash in the priest's throat. The priest struggles to catch his breath, choking on his own blood.

"Tesqua! Tesqua!" At the edge of the field an old man waves his arms and shouts in Cree, "Stop! Stop!" But Big Bear has no control here. Events have taken on a momentum of their own. Ignoring their chief, the men move in on her, tightening their circle till it seems she will be trampled. From the height of their horses, they loom over her, bodies painted yellow, porcupine quills jutting from black hair daubed with clay, feathers dangling from braids, faces streaked and dotted with black paint stare down at her.

Terrified, she backs away, desperately thrusting her hands in front of her as if to somehow push herself entirely from this field of slaughter, careful where she steps, looking over her shoulder to avoid tripping over another body . . .

"Theresa! Theresa!"

It is the Delaney woman, fifty feet away, kneeling between her dead husband and the black-robed body of Father Fafard. "Over here, Theresa!" she calls, standing up. They run to each other and in the comfort of their embrace shield themselves from the mounted Indians who surround them. Stopped by the women, the warriors lean out over their horses and watch them hold each other. They speak quietly in Cree while their idle horses stamp the melting snow and bend to snatch the grass uncovered by their hooves, in this the first moment of calm after the killings. Then a rider breaks from the circle, and shouting, waves his rifle across the creek to the Indian camp.

"Close your eyes and keep moving, Theresa," whispers the Delaney woman, still holding her, then breaking their embrace. "Be brave, for the water will be cold as ice."

Theresa Gowanlock holds her skirts high above water up to her knees, so cold the current cuts into her legs, numbing them until she can't move. She stands stock still in the middle of the creek, the cold current rushing against her legs. It comes to her now, as if she hears through the shock of the murders, his last words, spoken to her minutes ago, now, for the first time: he was sorry. He has left her alone in the world with his name, left her alone in this, and all he could say was he was sorry.

Someone is calling her name.

But Theresa Gowanlock cannot move out of the creek. There is nowhere to go. On one side, a field filled with corpses; on the other side, the Indian camp. No, she will simply stand here in the middle of the creek where it is safe.

A broken branch from an overhanging poplar floats by. She turns to watch it diminish downstream, a distant speck that bobs on the water, then disappears. She has become that small branch, a broken twig connected to nothing, caught in the eddies of a powerful current.

Someone is calling her name.

Stunned, she stands in the frigid water, the current pulling at her legs, refusing to move, realizing in the first minutes after the killings, what has happened. The shock recedes enough for her to regain a vague awareness, someone calling her.

"Tess! Tess!" the Delaney woman calls from the far shore. "Whatever are you doing out there?"

Beyond the creek, wisps of blue smoke drift upward between the lodgepoles of the Indian camp.

Theresa Gowanlock slowly moves forward through the water toward the women she first saw on the bridge at Battleford.

End of the Line

Vancouver-New Westminster, 1948

ALL ALONG THE LINE PASSENGERS GOT ON AND OFF at each station and to Cameron this was quite confusing, for though it seemed he was on a train, in fact he wasn't. Yes, this outfit had a conductor with a black uniform and hat like on a train, and this rig ran on rails like a train, but instead it was one self-contained rail car that ran on electricity connected to some overhead wires. And it was all windows, huge windows, the whole upper half of the car. The modern age. He watched the furtive hurry of the passengers and thought, technology is not wisdom. Then, in the stubborn manner of an old man who shut out anything he didn't like, he pretended he was on a real train anyway. After all, he thought, settling in, opening his briefcase and pulling out a sheaf of papers and photographs as if he had all the time in the world, I am going to the end of the line.

Cameron concentrated on the photographs spread out on his lap, all men he had known in another time. They were all gone now. John Pritchard, the half-breed interpreter, passing unnoticed, except by Cameron who thought he should have been decorated a hero for protecting the two white women in Big Bear's camp.

Wandering Spirit at the end of a rope in Battleford. Little Poplar in a gun fight two years later. Imasees in Montana for thirty years before getting a reservation for the people who had followed him there.

Cameron looked up from his photographs at the small boy and his young father seated across from him. To Cameron they lived in another world. Dressed in the bright stylish optimism emerging at the end of the Second World War, they would never know what he could never forget: that they lived and moved on this continent always at the expense of the people they had displaced. They will never see it, he thought, resting his head against the rattling window pane of the rail car, looking out at the settled countryside. Strings of new houses blurred by in the grey coastal drizzle, saddening him with the passage of time and the coming end of his own.

Of the white men at Frog Lake, Cameron alone had survived the massacre and he was eighty-three-years-old, a hold-over from another century, shuttling now between two cities on the Interurban somewhere between Vancouver and New Westminster. He had spent his entire life scuttling from city to city. Oh, he had tried to settle down, even to marry that girl working the dining hall of the hotel in Fort Frances. For a while she had traveled with him, once as far as Spokane, until things turned bad. She couldn't get used to his drifting from place to place, living from day to day, an itinerant hack who tried to make a living peddling his personal experiences to magazines for as little as three cents a word.

"The rate will be higher if you want the words arranged in sentences," quipped Cameron, but the editor was not amused and did not invite further submissions.

"A man proposing to make his living depending on the people who run our publications in Canada is a fit subject for a mental hospital," Cameron had once told Professor Morton.

Still, he had written the only book in existence on the Frog Lake Massacre, unless you counted those two women from Ontario who turned out that pathetic pamphlet that never would have been printed but for the fact Theresa Gowanlock's brother owned a press; that and a story someone ghosted for Eliza McLean in *The Beaver*.

It was forty-one years after the massacre when Ryerson published his manuscript in 1926. Then all he had to do was show up in any town or city with his illustrated lecture. Push the sales of the book. Give something of the events of Frog Lake and Pitt in '85. A little Indian sign language. Demonstrate a war dance. Chant some Cree. Light a fire with flint and steel. Why, it was a regular one-man Wild West show! And, of course, there were the lantern slides, the photographs . . .

Many of the photographs he was actually in himself, but then, that was what created so much interest in the book. The trick was to put in an appearance and get yourself photographed looking very much a part of things, like posing with Big Bear's twelve-year-old son, Horse Child, at Big Bear's trial.

Cameron, not wearing his own clothes at all but decked out as somebody's idea of a frontiersman, complete with an absurd hat, bandana, knife in belt, hands calmly folded over the business end of a Winchester; while Big Bear's son, looking quite lost, clutched some arrows and wondered where they had taken his father. That was the best one. It proved most useful and fetched top dollar. In fact, he had forgotten how many times he had resold the same photograph and now here it was again, some sixty years later, on page five of the *Saskatoon StarPhoenix*, a three-column feature sandwiched between an Old Virginia Pipe Tobacco ad and the movie playing at the Victory Theatre. BLEASDELL CAMERON, NOW 82, RETRACES PATH TAKEN BY BIG BEAR DURING REBELLION, and under the headline that same picture of him and Horse Child taken so long ago. At the Victory, John Garfield and Geraldine Fitzgerald were appearing with Walter Brennan and Faye Emerson in *Nobody Lives Forever*.

Well, that was certainly true, and it was good to see the movies had gotten something right for once, for as he pointed out to his friend Norman Luxton, movies were very much on his mind these days. Cameron had offered himself as a historical consultant to Cecil B. deMille for the movie North-West Mounted Police . . . this is just a whisper, but I may be going down to Hollywood, not to stay, of course, but I'm in touch with the local man of one of the big producing companies. We had a long talk this afternoon and he would like me either to go down there or to have one of their men come up and get in touch with me. He says I've got more good stuff on the West than all of Hollywood put together. This just happened through a friend who was with me in the mink venture. He happened to have known or met this motion picture man and told him about me and he took the matter up with his headquarters and today he got all the dope from me and will be writing them what he thinks they should do. So if I can get a trip to Hollywood with all expenses paid, why I'm for it . . .

Historical consultant, yes, that was the ticket. Let Luxton know he was keeping his hand in, had other things brewing, not nearly as desperate a situation as, in fact, it was. That way, when he tried to sell Luxton artifacts for the museum his friend was opening in Banff, he would get good prices. In the meantime he must start a project and extract some money from the history professor at the university, but he had to be careful for the professor had warned there were limits, once in a curious note at the bottom of a letter:

P.S. We do not wish to have a hundred applications for work like yours pour in upon us, so please make no mention of our arrangement.

Still if it was done right — pique some interest, vague and general with just enough detail to get the good professor going. He would write him a letter. Now here was a photograph for the professor! Cameron looking quite natty in a white suit and cap and mounted on a penny-farthing bicycle at the third annual Duck Lake Sports Day, 1891. And another taken that same Sports

Day, still dressed in his white suit and smiling benevolently while eighteen Indians glared at the ground as if the very earth itself had forsaken them and they had come to this, forced to tolerate this dandified white man because he happened to work for the Duck Lake Indian Agency. But they only barely tolerated the white man's presence. That was the hard lesson Cameron learned that bitter night on the ice at Frog Lake so long ago. Five days later, when their tolerance ran out, they killed every white man in the settlement but himself.

He was only twenty-two when it happened, but that day became the focal point of his entire life. As a detective pieces together clues to reconstruct the circumstances of a crime, so Cameron had reconstructed each minute of that day a thousand times. Still, after all this time, what actually happened seemed so incredible he could only grasp and accept it by carrying wherever he went these small tangible shreds of the day's occurrences.

Cameron's thumb and finger rubbed the corner of the tattered scrap of folded paper he removed from his waist-coat pocket, unfolded, and read Quinn's handwriting:

Dear Cameron,
Please give Miserable Man one blanket.
Thomas Trueman Quinn

It was not dated, there was no need; Cameron needed no mark to remember the date by.

He sat in the coach with the rhythm of the rails clacketing under him and as he read Quinn's note, a part of him was not in the coach at all, but reliving that Thursday, the day before Good Friday sixty-four years ago, when Wandering Spirit marked him for death and through a fluke set of circumstances he somehow escaped the fate of the others.

Three times that morning Wandering Spirit had tried to keep him with the others. "Why don't you go to church?" he asked, half-ordering Cameron to do so.

More insistent, the second time, barking the order at him: "Go to the instructor's house where the other whites are!"

Then exploding the third time: "I told you to stay with the other whites!"

Ah, but there was the small matter of a hat. Cameron was standing with an Indian named Yellow Bear on the hill a hundred yards from the Hudson's Bay store. "He's going with me to get a hat. The sun's hot and I have none," interjected Yellow Bear.

"Hurry back," ordered Wandering Spirit, and wheeling on his horse, galloped up the hill to Quinn's place.

A hat seems sane enough in all this madness, thought Cameron, walking to the Hudson's Bay store with Yellow Bear. The church was burning, the other whites were being herded into the field, and Yellow Bear, moved by some unaccountable whim, fancied a hat from the Bay store. Cameron turned the key in the door and, looking back over his shoulder, the last thing he saw before he and Yellow Bear stepped inside was

Wandering Spirit and Quinn facing each other on the crest of the hill. Yellow Bear began removing hats from the shelf, studiously trying each one on as if he had all the time in the world and nothing more important to do with it.

A loud rap on the door was followed by the entrance of Miserable Man, who silently thrust a note out from his huge bulk so Cameron could read it. It was the note from Quinn authorizing Cameron to give Miserable Man one blanket.

"I have no blankets," Cameron told him.

At length Miserable Man agreed to accept a shawl, some tea, and a twist of tobacco as a substitute. He was holding a corner of the shawl in each hand so that it formed a sack-like pouch into which Cameron was dropping first the tea and now the tobacco. A brown twist the size of a carrot, the tobacco landed softly in the pocket of the shawl at the precise moment the first shot, muffled by distance and the walls of the store, reached the three men inside.

Behind the counter, Yellow Bear stared into the upturned empty crown of the hat. Miserable Man froze, his pitted face inches from Cameron's, the eyes of both men locked as they counted off each crack of the rifle. On the third shot Miserable Man sprang into action. Quickly closing the shawl and tying the tea and tobacco in a bundle, he bolted from the shop. Cameron and Yellow Bear followed to the open doorway and searched the hillside where Wandering Spirit and Quinn had been standing. Wandering Spirit was riding down the hill, yelling in Cree to his followers in the field below.

Quinn lay dead on the ground. As Cameron folded the note Quinn had written him minutes ago, it was easy to imagine what had happened, Wandering Spirit ordering Quinn to join the others, just as he had ordered Cameron, Quinn refusing. The only difference between himself and Quinn was that Quinn did not have Yellow Bear to intervene. Quinn was dead and Cameron wasn't. The hat from the Bay store was just a pretext for Yellow Bear to get him away from Wandering Spirit and save him from the murders. The kindly Cree gripping Cameron by the wrist wasn't even wearing a hat now. "We must get you to the camp. Come this way," he urged.

Somewhere just outside New Westminster Cameron fell asleep.

In his dream Yellow Bear was guiding him through a field of corpses.

"End of the line, oldtimer!" The conductor tried to shake the old man awake.

Yellow Bear was taking Cameron to the safety of the neutral Woods Cree camp. When they were crossing the field after the shootings, Cameron insisted they stop to examine the corpses. He recognized George Dill's boots as they walked toward the body that lay face down in the field, the toes of his boots pointing inward and almost touching, heels angled out in the form of a V. Cameron turned him over, the face frozen in an expression of shocked surprise by the bullet that had stopped Dill in the back. Brown blades of last year's grass, twigs, and flecks of dirt were pressed into his forehead. As he looked into the lifeless face of his friend and former partner, Cameron wondered why he alone was spared.

"End of the line!" The conductor shook the old man again. Jesus — papers and photographs strewn all over the seat. The old guy must have fallen asleep. "End of the line!"

While struggling to recall and sustain the image, Cameron began to emerge from his dream. "Why me?" he wondered out loud.

The conductor had no idea what the old man was talking about. "You'll have to get off now," he said.

The British Columbia Electric Railway interurban trolley clanked and shunted into its New Westminster terminal.

Where was he? Banff? Yes, that was it. Going to see his friend Norman Luxton. He pressed his face against the window and looked out into the terminal. No, certainly not Banff. Cameron was too proud to ask the conductor where he was and even if he knew, he wouldn't know why he was here. Not that it mattered. He was an old man living from day to day, hand to mouth, on the move so many years now that everything had begun to blur into a desperate sameness. Well, thought Cameron, scooping the newspapers and photographs off the seat and stuffing them in his briefcase, it would certainly all come clear with time.

Confused, and not yet fully awake, he was just stepping down off the train with a leather bag in one hand and a briefcase stuffed with papers in the other. God, it was awkward, being a one-man travelling medicine show, packing everything with him everywhere he went. He'd actually done that in the thirties, hawked medicine, but he was on top of things again now because after all this time the book was about to be reprinted, thanks largely to Luxton.

Look at that, pure heaven: the coal black, brushed-out hair of a woman standing with her back to him in the terminal. No harm in looking, surely. That was all he'd been able to do for over fifteen years, just look. A little like getting on a train and forgetting where he was going, and why, but hoping it would come to him eventually.

Now as he stood at the top of the step-well, he realized he was not on the train, but on a trolley in New Westminster. No doubt something would soon trigger his memory of why he was here.

She turned toward him and he was looking at her as he stepped down from the trolley and felt, too late, his descending foot miss the step. He flung his hand with the briefcase out in front of him to brace the fall; his head struck the concrete.

A small crowd was gathering. He could feel people hovering over him, but he couldn't move, couldn't get up. Someone was calling an ambulance.

In the hospital again, this time the Department of Veterans Affairs in New Westminster. How embarrassing, and worse, he didn't know how he'd gotten here. He had a concussion, a sore ankle, and the doctor talked about a bruised kidney, whatever that was. Well, he felt perfectly fine, and if they insisted on keeping him here for a few weeks, he'd just catch up on his correspondence and get some work done.

First there was Luxton. He wanted to send Norman some artifacts for his Indian museum in lieu of payment on loans his friend had made to him, a delicate matter which he would approach indirectly so that it never seemed he was selling the artifacts to Luxton, even though he really was.

Dear Norman:

This will be a short letter for the light is bad. I am writing you from the hospital where I have been momentarily detained with nothing more serious than a sore ankle. I don't know how I hurt it unless it was getting on and off those crowded street cars. You come down on the hard pavement like a ton of brick, but don't worry, I'm on the mend and expect to get out of here soon.

While I think of it, I want to send you a big well-made and inlaid Sioux redstone pipe, and also, a beaded coup stick. I will be sending you the pipe and coup stick this week and I hope to square up your loan to me soon. I saw the other day that some Indian Institute or organization in New York has paid $500 for an Indian pipe.

Please excuse this terrible scrawl which I hope you can read. I've forgotten how to write with a pen and this is the worst fountain pen but the only one I could get a hold of here in the hospital.

Well Norman, old friend, all the best to you.

Heartily yours,
W.B. Cameron

Sending Norman a few things to put in his Banff Indian Trading Post would help keep the peace. Even if he couldn't pay off his debt in cash, Cameron could fill Luxton's entire museum with artifacts; he'd been trading with the Indians for years. Long before people like Luxton were opening their Indian Trading Post in Banff, Cameron had been at the vanguard of white collectors. Once the Indians had been conquered and swindled out of their land, there was nothing left to take from them but their culture. Hell, it made sense in a warped kind of way, and no sooner had the hostiles surrendered than Cameron was back in the Indian camp with a trading outfit and in one day secured most of their saleable property.

Once a trader, always a trader, and when he'd accumulated all their possessions and the Indians had nothing left to trade, he became a journalist. For what does a journalist do but live off what happens to other people? And Cameron was right there for all of it, even the hangings. His was the only authentic eyewitness account of the massacre and its aftermath. He was there. That's what made it such a fine piece of frontier journalism.

And now, after all these years, Luxton and some people in Calgary were having the book reprinted. Why, then, was he now having second thoughts about it all? He had made the fatal mistake of writing about himself, his actual experiences, his life, and now in his final years he wondered whether in so doing, he had not somehow cheapened and diminished it.

For years the massacre had remained a mystery to him. No matter how he looked at the killings, they didn't make sense. Once while editing a newspaper in Bassano he met an old Blackfoot woman who claimed religion was at the root of the massacre: Wandering Spirit's behaviour in the church, the killing of the priests, the burning of the church. They were testing the white man's religion, testing its power. But the woman herself had been raised by nuns and later became involved in Native religion, so naturally her point of view would be religious. No, there was no rational explanation for the killings at Frog Lake.

So it had seemed. But lately his perspective was changing, his sympathies shifting. He was beginning to see things differently. A selfish and corrupt government intent on pushing the railroad through and pushing Big Bear and his people off the plains. Delaney and Quinn had cooked up a scheme that had the Indians clearing the land they planned to sell for homesteads. Gowanlock would take the logs at his mill.

Then too, Delaney abused his power as Farm Instructor to take advantage of Indian women. When the husband of one of the women protested, a man named Sand Fly, John Delaney trumped up charges of assault against him, had him imprisoned, and then cohabited with his wife all winter. To add insult to injury, when he tired of the Indian woman, Delaney married a white woman, Theresa Delaney.

So the massacre. The provocation, Cameron concluded, while it did not excuse, was some mitigation of the wrongdoings.

Still, no point in brooding about it now; he had another letter to write. When Cameron stayed in a hotel he was in the habit of taking as much hotel stationery as he could lay his hands on, and then using it indiscriminately. As most of Cameron's letters were about money, the first thing he had to do was cross out the letterhead and address on the stationery. Otherwise the desired funds ended up sitting in some mail slot in a hotel lobby thousands of miles from where he actually was. Cameron reached into the bag on his table and pulled a sheet of paper from a substantial stationery collection that spanned the many years he had kicked around the country.

	HOTEL ALEXANDRA	
Rates $1.50 and $2.00 Per Day With Private Bath $2.50 Telephone M 4671	**FIREPROOF** F.G. Hughes and H. Corry, Lessees and Managers Calgary, Alta.	Fully Licensed Free Bus All Modern Conveniences

As Cameron struck out the address on the letterhead, he realized the stationery was exactly twenty-four years older than the date he was now writing on it.

He must now include an address where he would be able to receive a reply two weeks from now. Where would he be? Still in the hospital? Or in Banff . . .

Calgary . . . Regina . . . Saskatoon? He didn't know and the doctors would give no indication of when he would be released.

Cameron placed the pen and paper on the night table, lay back in his bed, and turned out the light. Then it came to him.

It didn't matter anymore.

A NEON SIGN ZAPPED and sputtered in the pre-dawn drizzle.

WILD WAVES AMAZING KINGDOM OF THE SEA
GIANT 40 POUND SALMON
WHALE WATCHING
TACKLE
BOATS
GUIDES

Flashlight beams wobbled as men hurried by him in the dark. Wilson, the fisherman's friend and guide was awake and working at four o'clock in the morning.

Two men looked out a window, switched off a television, rattled the aluminum door of an RV shut, and emerged carrying a large tackle box and fishing rods.

"I'm Elton and this here's Wendell. We never seen an ocean and we sure never seen no forty pound chinook salmon!"

"'cept on teevee," corrected Wendell. "We mostly fish bass stateside, but we seen a show on teevee about the giant forty pound chinook salmon at Wild Waves."

Wilson's first sighting of a salmon was a distant memory. In those days, they raked herring fingerlings for bait. Just a boy then, when he shut off the four horse Briggs-Stratton engine, the only sound the sea lapping the sides of a fourteen foot cedar boat gliding through kelp. He would stand poised and ready to slice the wafer-thin blade of the herring rake into the bright blue-green sea. Ribbons of kelp parting beneath the boat's cutting bow and there, below him, the dappled beauty of the wild salmon at rest in its element; and then sensing the boat above, with a slight waver of its tail the salmon darted from sight.

"C'mon boys!" Wilson urged his clients across the plain of crushed rock that formed the breakwater for Wild Waves Marina and the campsite for the motorhomes and trailers they were walking between.

"Let's see if we can catch the first light and a closer look at that salmon."

"Alright!" whooped Elton.

The hot pink hootchy lure glowed in the dark as a northwesterly wind turned the flasher on its swivel. Line taut from tip to reel, the flasher banged and jangled at the tip of Elton's rod.

"Watch your step," cautioned Wilson.

The smell of the sea grew stronger as they made their way down the cleats of a marina ramp slick with rain.

Onboard, his clients were passengers, not crew, so he was alarmed to see Elton unfasten the lines holding the boat to the dock. Wilson rushed forward to start the engine as the boat drifted in the crowded marina.

"We underway yet?" asked Wendell.

The starter snarled and whined, the boat drifted, and then the engine fired and caught, stuttering to life.

"Yes," said Wilson. "We are underway."

The steady pop-pop-pop of the engine exhaust trailed behind them. The boat slipped past the breakwater, and Wilson held his course in the crowded moving lights of cabin cruisers and bayliners.

One thing about guiding, it had kept him on the water all these years. Maybe that's what it was really about, not the fish, but the peace that came from being on the water.

Clearing the buoy beyond the dock, he swung hard to port and opened throttle. Boats were all around him, only their navigation lights visible in the darkness. Skimming across the black water like comets in the sky, the boats sped toward a single point, his own becoming another moving light converging on the cape. Every year there were more fishermen and fewer fish.

It was almost noon now and Wilson and his two clients were crammed in a flotilla jockeying for position to troll the length of a reef where any remaining chinook salmon might be feeding.

With so many boats fishing the same water, an unspoken code of traffic rules had evolved; three or four boats abreast in each direction, like right and left lanes of traffic; three lines trolling from each boat, the boats crowded so close together the slightest variation in speed or direction could create a havoc of crossed lines and flared tempers.

They were entering the most congested area now, and as Wilson locked his speed consistent with the boats in front, behind, and on each side, he felt himself being caught in something out of his control.

Elton and Wendell sat across from one another astern, each holding a rod out.

"Hell!" cursed Elton, as Wilson swerved to avoid colliding with an off course cabin cruiser. "This ain't no salmon derby. It's a demolition derby!"

Boats passed so close people conversed from one to the other.

"You could walk across this channel, stepping from boat to boat," complained Elton. "I don't believe this. We drive all the way up into Canada for our great natural outdoor getaway and what do we get? It's like we never left home. Or we did, and dragged the same old shit up here with us."

"Well, didn't we?" asked Wendell, who up to this point had said nothing.

"What do you mean?"

Even though Wilson kept out of conversations between his clients, in the enclosed space of his boat he couldn't help overhearing that the brothers were on the verge of a quarrel.

"Well, we drove mother's monster motorhome all the way up I-5. And there's hundreds of campers hooked up at Wild Waves just like ours, towing the same old shit, dumping the same old shit. I mean, they have a waste disposal station at Wild Waves where we drive up, and unload our shit. So, yeah, I figure we did kinda drag the same old shit up here."

"Shh!" Elton put his finger to his lips and whispered. "Fish don't like bad karma."

"Fish? Don't make me laugh."

"It's true. I seen it on a nature show on teevee, The Knowledge Network."

"It wasn't The Knowledge Network. It was The Learning Channel. TLC. That's where we saw it. The Learning Channel."

"Anyways, salmon are the most evolved fish on the planet. They migrate to the sea and live in the ocean for three, four years, before returning to the exact same stream they were born in to lay their eggs in the gravel bed and then die. So, if they can do all that, find their way out of the ocean back to the stream where they were born, they certainly can sense bad vibes, don't you think?"

"No. I don't. But if, for just a minute, your theory is true, there won't be any salmon within miles of this sorry-assed scene."

Wilson had been listening and knew they were right. Three men with baseball caps on backwards raised their beer cans as they trolled past in an open aluminum boat so close he could've jumped into it. They were in a sea of boats, a crowd looking for the big one, and not finding it, becoming ugly.

Two complete passes off the rock, first one direction, then the other, the morning almost over and no action on the rods. Wilson went forward and stood over the bow, studying the water. Elton took the wheel through the turn.

"I got one!" yelled Wendell, his rod bending 'til the tip touched the water.

"Hey! Watch where you're going!" someone yelled from the bayliner ahead.

They were no longer running parallel with the other boats but across their path at an angle.

"It's a big one!" Wendell yelled.

A man stepped out of the cabin of the bayliner and shook his fist. "I'm warning you . . . "

Locked on a collision course, the big bayliner loomed closer. The man yelling at them wore an olive and brown camouflage suit. He cradled a rifle under his right arm, and his left hand gripped the railing as he leaned out over it shouting, "Get outa my way dickhead!"

The barrel of the rifle angled over the railing, the muzzle pointed down at Wilson's boat. Wilson grabbed the wheel, put the boat in reverse, and waited for the braking effect to kick in.

"It's a big one!" yelled Wendell, his rod bent double. "Hey! What're you doing?"

Wilson grabbed the tip of Wendell's rod and slashed his knife blade through the line. The rod sprang straight and the line lay slack on the water.

He didn't have time to explain to an American bass fisherman who watched too much television that he'd hooked the tackle trolled from the bayliner. In the cabin he set the throttle on full and watched the boats recede.

Once it had been wooden clinkers with five horse Briggs-Stratton inboards. In a space so small it was difficult to stand, he had sat on a plank seat, rod between his legs, and trailed a buck-tail in the boat's wake or trolled a dimpled brass and nickel Tom Mack $4^{1/2}$ spoon.

Now it was high-tech rednecks, downriggers, depth finders, bayliners and, it seemed, guns. Someone had aimed a rifle at him and the salmon were gone. It was time to get out. It felt like the end of something, the end of a way of life.

"Ecotourism will be the new wave, and there will always be room for a new wave at Wild Waves," proclaimed his boss.

"Next season there'll be more salmon than ever. I'm farming them. Aqua-culture. Anyone who buys salmon in a supermarket is eating farm salmon raised in pens and fed food pellets."

"What's salmon farming got to do with salmon fishing?" asked Wilson.

"Give me a minute and I'll show you." His boss was up out of his chair now, in front of his desk, rearranging things on it.

"Look," he said. "We've already got a huge pool facility here and this winter I'm having it enlarged and stocked with farm raised salmon. Now, just imagine this desk is the pool, and these paper clips are boats."

The owner of Wild Waves busily lined up paper clips along the edge of his desk and began hooking them together. "See, we run a series of small boats around the perimeter of the pool."

He moved the front paper clip with his finger and the connected paper clips moved along the edge of his desk. "Boats guided on cables running on tracks laid on the bottom of the pool. No collisions. No nasty incidents like your episode yesterday. These guys won't even steer. They just pay to get into the boat and dangle rods overboard 'til they snag one of our farm raised salmon. Salmon fishing will become the latest ride in the Wild Waves amusement park. I think I'll place it between the Tilt-A-Whirl and the water chutes. What do you think, Wilson? Wilson? Come back here. Don't you want to be part of the new wave?"

But Wilson was gone. By mid-afternoon he was driving aimlessly on the backroads, beyond the strip malls and tourist traps, where he could still find traces of the island he grew up on.

He parked and got out into an autumn afternoon rain, walking the riverbank between the bridge and the train trestle, the river swollen with fall runoff. The steelhead are extinct now but a few salmon have returned to spawn and die. White bare-bone skeletons float in the shallows, and the gray skins, pecked clean by the gulls, hang like ragged cloth from the roots of the stumps that line the bank.

Upstream, a fisherman is wading into the middle of the river to cast into water pooling in backeddies. The moment and precise angle when the rod becomes an extension of the man's arm thrust out over the water, the line unfurls over his head, further and further across the river, the fly at the end of the uncoiling line landing in the pool. Over and over the man places his fly in precisely the same spot in the pool.

The figure of the man casting into a river where there are no fish, haunts him. What is he fishing for? Some remnant of his past that can never be recovered? Himself?

The current pulls at his legs, drawing him further into the river.

A GREEN GLOW EMANATED FROM THE GRAPHITE DASH as Susan and Craig floated in the Grand's muffled comfort on the snow-packed winding mountain road.

Last winter, Cabos San Lucas; this winter, Whistler. The great Canadian ski holiday. Susan wanted to fly but Craig insisted they take their new GMA. The Grand Millenium Adventurer, he hastened to remind her, was the ultimate sport-utility vehicle.

"I thought we agreed we wouldn't just take holidays. We'd have experiences. Well, this is our chance."

"Chance?"

"To test the GMA. Really go somewhere. Off-trail. Virgin snow."

And plenty of it. Not even trees. Just the white contour of their tops buried beneath snow. But the exchange rate was good and you didn't have to put up with beach pedlars and bandits. Still, she missed the sun.

She found the Grand's overhead console unit a little unsettling simply because it was overhead. Or was it just over *her* head?

There was a computer up there, a compass, an outside temperature display, and a transmitter of some kind. The computer was handy and knowing the outside temperature was interesting — minus thirteen right now — but she found the digital compass read-out constantly flashing its changing direction down on her an annoying irrelevance.

"I don't get it," she said. "We're coming around this curve and the compass reads 180 degrees north. Then when we're round the curve we're headed north west, then west, but wait, here comes another curve in the road, south this time. So where are we? And where are we going? There's no way of knowing unless we stop because the direction's always changing. But when we stop, we're not going anywhere, so it doesn't matter."

"You really don't get it do you? The compass is for off-road use."

He was adopting his male superior technical tone and she didn't want to listen to another lecture justifying why they needed a fifty thousand dollar sport-utility vehicle.

"Off-road?" she said. "Why would we ever drive off the road? Isn't that how accidents happen? I thought the whole point of driving was to stay on the road, not drive off it."

Too much, thought Craig, opting for silence while the quartz halogen headlights and the perfect control of the four-wheel drive tracked them through the turn that followed the curved shore of the frozen lake on his side, a solid bank of snow on hers.

Overhead, the compass flashed digital bytes that marked the mad flux of the curve. Craig gripped the wheel with both hands and followed the tracks of the vehicle ahead. As the GMA unwound through the turn, the tire treads ahead crossed into the oncoming lane, the four-wheel drive holding the road, and then, dead ahead, a man and woman stood on the road, upraised hands shielding their eyes from the blinding glare of the Grand's headlights. A mattress lay across the oncoming lane; an overturned pickup truck, its canopied roof squashed into the snow, the side of the truck crumpled into the snowbank.

"There's been an accident Craig. Stop!"

"Can't stop in the middle of the road. Cause a pile-up." He imagined his silver lacquered pride flattened into scrap. "I'll pull in behind."

A cloud of steam seeped from under the hood and hung in the sub-zero air above the overturned truck. A green pool of antifreeze spread across the road toward the mattress that lay in the oncoming lane of the snow-packed ice clad highway. The door of the cab of the truck was ajar, where they climbed out, Craig guessed.

"What happened?" he asked.

Dazed in the white glare of the headlights, the man stared straight past him into the oncoming lane, as if looking for an answer.

"Don't know," he said. "Happened so fast."

"We should get this mattress off the road," said Craig.

Within the warmth of the GMA, Susan watched Craig talking to the other man, his breath turning to fog as he spoke. Sometimes to her he seemed like a little boy with his new toys, looking for adventure. Well, she thought, he's found it now.

Craig bent over the mattress, and pushed it off the road. When he got it to the side of the road he gave it one last shove. The mattress slid down the embankment and out onto the snow where it was finally stopped by the soft fresh snow plowing ahead of it. He got no help from the man who stood motionless staring into space.

"We can take you to the nearest town," offered Craig. "Or you can stay here, and we'll send help out for you, an ambulance, tow truck, notify the police . . . "

"No need!" the man suddenly shouted. "We'll take the ride!"

He thrust his hand out at Craig. "Name's Delwin. Some call me Del, some call me Win, but my real name is Delwin. That's my wife, Dianne."

He pointed at the rear of a woman in tight jeans wriggling into the back of the overturned truck. Now she was backing out of the truck with two garbage bags she set down at the side of the road.

Delwin and Dianne. Easy enough to remember. "I'm Craig Mathews. My wife Susan is in the GMA and you better get Dianne inside it, too. Anything you want to take out of your truck right now? I mean, you'll be coming back here with a tow truck later, but still . . . "

"Nah. Just leave it."

"Delwin!" The woman called, as she walked toward the GMA. "Don't you forget the bags!"

"We've got to get off this highway," said Craig. "This is a perfect set up for the next car coming along to pile into us. How much luggage have you got in the truck?"

"Just these, that's all." He lifted one of the garbage bags but before he could get the other, Craig had grabbed it and the two men were walking toward the rear of the GMA.

Craig's thumb touched the control pad and the rear hatch opened. "The GMA can seat eight but the last pair of seats is folded down right now. That's where we'll stow your bags."

Craig lifted one of the garbage bags into the luggage compartment and Delwin followed. Stacked neatly in a corner, the tightly tied olive green bags blended into the forest green interior of the GMA.

"Those bags are sure light," remarked Craig.

"Travelling light," said Delwin.

With his control pad, Craig closed the rear hatch and opened the side door. Delwin took the seat next to his wife Dianne. Craig was already sitting behind the steering wheel but the side door was shutting on its own.

"This is . . . " Delwin found himself enclosed inside an environment utterly foreign and fantastic. "This is . . . "

"The new GMA."

"GMA?"

"The Grand Millenium Adventurer," said Craig, tilting Delwin's seat back. "We call it the Grand. About fifty grand."

"Ah," said Delwin, sinking into the seat's ergonomic cocoon. "That one."

He himself drove a 1968 half-ton truck that kept running because he could always find used parts in the wrecking yards. You could buy whole engines at wrecking yards. So far he had installed three wrecking yard engines in the truck that now lay overturned at the side of the highway, increasingly far behind them.

The woman had turned around to look at him. "You've had an acci*dent*," she said, emphasizing the last syllable. "You must be cold. Can I get you both something warm to drink?"

"Got any coffee?" asked Dianne.

"I could fix you a latte."

Delwin had never had one but through some sudden turn in fortune found himself inside the Grand Millenium Adventurer where a latte was now being offered to him. "That would be fine," he said.

"We bought the Grand on the net," said Susan over the hiss of an espresso machine.

"Thank you," said Delwin, holding the warm foaming cup in his hand. "What was that about a net?"

"No. We bought it on the net. www.car.com. We just kept clicking the mouse and three days later the dealer showed up with the Grand in our driveway."

"Mind if I smoke?" asked Dianne.

"Must you?" Susan said.

"Nerves. We were just about killed back there. I'm still shaking."

"Oh, I see," said Susan. "Well I . . . "

"It's alright," interjected Craig. "Each seat has a separate air conditioning module. You can exist in an entirely different environment than that of the person next to you."

She must be in her early twenties, Susan thought, watching the woman's right hand scramble and grope in her purse, the fingers of her left hand touching the inside of her brassiere, all the while looking at Susan with green eyes speckled with grey.

"Far out," she said, pleased to have found what she was looking for, or perhaps commenting on Craig's description of the air conditioning. Susan glanced at Craig. You never knew what people meant when they used language like that.

Dianne removed a hand-rolled cigarette from inside her brassiere, and wet its pinched end between her lips, while her right hand produced a lighter from her purse. She lit the end and Susan watched her face squeeze in concentration while she sucked in smoke till the tip glowed red. Lips pursed closed, she held in the fumes a full minute and then exhaled, all the while looking at Susan as cannabis smoke curled from her nostrils and mouth, filling the interior of the Grand.

"Here," she said, smoke pouring from her open mouth as she offered the joint to Susan.

"No! No!" said Susan. "I thought you meant cigarettes!"

She turned to Craig. "This woman pulls dope out of her brassiere and smokes it in our brand new GMA, and I want to know what you are going to do about it!"

In the back seat Dianne smoked her joint down to a roach ringed with resin, frowned when it went out, and deposited the remains in a small tin box marked Celestial Seasonings Herbal Tea.

"This is my fault," Craig said. "Showing off. Telling everyone about the Grand's air conditioning."

"Well, let's just hope it really works," said Susan.

"Why?" asked Craig. "What are you talking about?"

He pressed the air purifier module but the computerized controls, ducts, and venting, could not control the fumes from the powerful hydroponically-grown pot. Smoke filled the interior of the GMA, transforming it into a giant bong on wheels in which they were all enclosed.

"Second-hand smoke. I'm talking about second-hand smoke," said Susan. "I feel funny. We'd better stop at the next town."

"This sure beats sleeping on a mattress in the back of our old truck!" Dianne bounced on the Travelodge bed, flipping channels. CNN, TLC, CBC Local News. "Del. There's our truck! On TV!"

On the television, a woman wearing a winter parka stood in front of Delwin and Dianne's truck and spoke into a microphone. "What happened here on this deserted stretch of snowbound highway earlier this evening remains a mystery." The woman's blonde head turned toward the overturned truck. "Road conditions here are extremely hazardous and apparently the driver lost control and the truck overturned. No one was found at the scene, leaving police to speculate on the whereabouts and condition of the driver and any passengers. Back to you, Ken."

"Thanks, Catherine. You said passengers. How many people do the police think were in the truck?"

"We don't know, Ken. Some clothing and personal items suggest a couple, but there's really no way of knowing at this point."

"Thanks for that, Catherine. We have just learned that the overturned truck may have been driven by Del and Dee Dee O'Connor, currently being sought by police on undisclosed charges. Police are warning drivers not to pick up hitchhikers. The couple may be dangerous."

"Turn that thing off, will you?" said Delwin. "If they hear it, or if they're watching television in the next room, we're done. Finished."

Dianne aimed the remote at the screen like it was a gun.

Delwin put his ear against the wall. "It's O.K." he said. "They don't have the television on. They're just talking."

"What are they saying?"

"I can't really make anything out."

"Try," she said. "Try real hard."

"You really did it this time, Craig. Two professionals looking for a little rest and relaxation, a winter holiday, but you have to turn it into a big adventure. I hope you're satisfied."

"Well what was I supposed to do? Let them off back there in the middle of the night. Nothing was open."

"That woman is breaking the law."

"It's different up here in Canada. They don't put people in jail for smoking pot. I read about it in the *Atlantic*."

"I don't care what your liberal magazine says, Craig. It's wrong. That woman can't see straight. You know what she told me?"

"No."

"She's pregnant. Yes, pregnant. She'll be lucky if the baby isn't born malformed with all the toxins in her system. If she even carries it to term."

"I don't know where you come up with this stuff."

"Mothers. It's mother's stuff. I don't like drugs," said Susan. "Drugs are for people who can't handle reality."

"Maybe it's the other way around," offered Craig, turning his back to her and pulling at the bed covers.

"Meaning?" snapped Susan.

"Reality is for people who can't handle drugs."

"I just wish I had some of my things from the truck."

"Like what?" Delwin watched her cross her arms and lift her T-shirt over her head.

"That aquamarine nightgown would be nice. It's your favourite isn't it?"

"Well, what were we supposed to do?" Delwin paced back and forth, trying to stay focussed while the woman he loved was undressing. "Hang around and wait in some small town for a week to get the truck repaired. Even if we managed to stay out of jail it would cost thousands of dollars to get that junker on the road again. You heard the television." He pointed at the blank screen.

"We've disappeared. We've ditched the truck and taken on a whole new identity. My only regret about this so-called accident is that you told me to bring those bags and I was stupid enough to do it. I really feel we have a chance here, but we're driving around with enough high-grade dope to get all of us into serious trouble."

"Stop thinking bad thoughts about those garbage bags and think of them as assets."

"Assets?"

"Do you think I asked you to bring those bags along just so I could smoke that shit? I couldn't smoke all that pot in a lifetime. There's enough high-grade hydroponic in those bags to stone a city. And it's worth a lot of money. Anyhow, if it makes you nervous, just pretend it isn't there and you won't be so on edge."

"Pretend it isn't there? Jesus!" How could you argue with logic like that. "Dianne, what if we get caught? What will we do then, pretend it isn't there?"

"That's right. That's exactly right. And the reason we'll pretend it isn't there is because we don't know anything about it. It's not ours. It's theirs. Anyone asks, those two bags belong to them, not us."

"What do you think those two bags are worth?" he asked.

"Hard to say right off. Have to check the market. It's worth a lot of money in the States. Course we'd have to get it there wouldn't we?"

"There?"

"Our two bags. Across the border."

"How much? Take a guess."

"I'll bet it's worth just as much as their precious GMA."

"The Grand? Fifty thousand dollars!"

"Probably. So you see, we're just as well off as them. It's all a matter of perspective. If we play our cards right, we could end up with the Grand and the two bags. Are you with me, Delwin?"

He was watching her eyes change colour, the range of her moods mirrored in shifting shades of green. Like silt mingling with the Pacific Ocean at the river's mouth where the water is always changing, becoming a darker green further from the shore, just so, her eyes were always changing.

"Good. Because I'm there, honey. I can almost see it."

Her eyes had drained of colour to a washed out pale and sickly yellow. Green eyes gone dead.

"Tomorrow I want you to talk to Craig about taking us across the border," she said.

"That's impossible. How did we end up in this?"

"Good karma. Think good thoughts and it will happen. We'll make it happen."

"Good thoughts? What kind of good thoughts?"

"C'mere 'babe. I'll show you."

Later, as he reached over to turn out the lamp on her side of the bed, as he bent over the woman, vulnerable in her sleep, her long brown hair flowing across his pillow, she seemed to him to be like a child again.

He switched out the light and lay on his back in the darkness, listening to her breathe beside him, feeling the warmth of her body glow with an incredible appetite for life. What shade of green were her eyes when she slept? he wondered. No one knew. No one would ever know.

Who is she? wondered Susan, next morning at breakfast, intrigued, envying her youth. Pretty in a rough kind of Huck Finn way. A thin slash of scar tissue hooked under her lip in a white half-moon curve the size of a thumbnail. And eyes. Every time Susan looked into them they were changing colour. Green eyes flecked with grey and brown. Who indeed? wondered Susan, amazed, listening to the girl talk about life on the road.

"Last time we were in an accident, I was asleep through the whole thing, Del trying to make time driving through while I slept on the mattress in the back of the truck. Anyhow, he needed a coffee to stay awake, so he pulled into some little all-night gas station, got out of the truck, left it running in neutral, and went inside, me asleep all the while in the back, and when he came out with his coffee the truck wasn't where he'd left it, the truck was coasting on the slope of the asphalt, rolling backwards and out of control. From where he stood holding his coffee, he watched our truck narrowly miss the only other car in the parking lot, veer by a metal lamp post, roll out onto a highway where transport trucks roared by in both directions, across the highway, and come to a stop in a snowbound ditch. Luckily the gas station had a tow truck. That's what woke me up, the jerking motion of the steel cable on the tow truck winching our truck out of the ditch. I'd slept through the whole thing. Not a scratch, just like when we jackknifed the trailer. Remember Del?"

Remember? Jesus. How could he forget! Because each terrifying second could have been their last, he could recall each detail of that near fatal accident, so long ago, in the present, as if it was happening right now, while he was sitting in the Travelodge restaurant eating breakfast.

. . . it begins with a wobble in the steering wheel. Something trying to pull the wheel from side to side. Like the truck needs front end work. Only now, it's worse. The front end shakes like it's shot, the trailer veers from side to side on the highway, and he's hanging onto the wheel with both hands.

Delwin glances in the mirror, sees the trailer veer across the highway; looks in the mirror again, the trailer's back where it's supposed to be, behind the truck. The wheel jerks in his hands and the trailer veers onto the curb.

The weight of Dianne's grandmother's wood cook stove causing the trailer to zig-zag all over the road, the car behind honking, the driver going nuts, trapped behind a trailer swinging back and forth on its ball hitch. Fishtailing. A lopsided Just Married *sign pinned to a trailer fishtailing down the highway.*

An oncoming car swerves onto the shoulder to avoid hitting them. Spraying gravel on their windshield, the driver speeds on by wondering what he so narrowly missed.

Why it's two people enclosed in a steel capsule hurtling down the highway with an out-of-control trailer overloaded with grandma's stove, the steering wheel wobbling so bad he doesn't know if he can hold it.

If he keeps his hands on the wheel he'll have a better chance at control but the car and trailer are taking on an energy and momentum of their own, sudden and irreversible.

Four wheel drift.

Get down on the floor, Dianne. Scrunch down under the dash. Real quick!

The trailer wrenches off its ball hitch and slams into the cab. The door where Dianne is crouched crumples in against her as the truck caroms off a bank and bounces to a rest, wedged between the jackknifed trailer and the embankment.

That was how they found them, banging on the window of the truck cab. And yes, he remembers that near fatal accident in the present, because the helpless feeling of losing control remains a constant in his life.

It had started well. He remembered ordering from the seed catalogue.

Hawaiian.

The Hawaiian is a pure sativa originating from the big island of Mauna Kea. It's been bred and stabilized for more than 15 years on Vancouver Island. Sugary with crystal, it has a very distinctive citrus odour and menthol flavour that tingles the taste buds and tickles the brain. Tall vigorous growth with few branches, classic cactus shape. Extreme elongation in the first two weeks of flowering with tufts of long thin hairs developing into long sticky spear buds which thicken up after the sixth or seventh week. The lemon flavour intensifies when flushed for a long time(3 weeks) with straight water. Very energetic and up high, great to smoke during the day for an active lifestyle.

Flowering Period: 10-12 wks

Harvesting went well enough. Stalks stripped, leaves, tops, piled high and drying, everything fine 'til Dianne discovered a recipe for distilling the stalks into oil, which is exactly what she was doing when the explosion from the alcohol on the stove blew the back wall out of the kitchen and started a fire in the house. The end of everything they'd worked for. Grab two garbage bags and run, and they'd been running ever since.

Sitting here this morning in the Travelodge restaurant, he realized it was not Dianne's grandmother's stove that caused the trailer to jackknife, or the alcohol to explode in the kitchen. In some way, he knew, it was Dianne herself. Living with Dianne was like hanging onto the steering wheel in the middle of four wheel drift, a scary ride that could get you killed, an accident, Susan would say. The alcohol in a hash oil still explodes on their stove. Jesus. It could have killed them both.

"What's the matter, Del?" asked Dianne. "You don't look so good."

"Too much coffee. I'll be right back."

Like many males, Craig did not share his habit with Susan, and Delwin and Dianne's dope was now driving a wedge between them. In the gated community in which Craig and Susan lived, purchasing drugs was a complicated process in which you paid money to keep your distance from the source. Here, it seemed more open, and Craig's sense of enlightenment and general well being was further enhanced that very afternoon by a direct hit off Dianne and Delwin's hydroponic.

"Right on," said Craig, inhaling the proffered joint. "Righteous," he said, exhaling. "Righteous weed."

It was indeed, as the seed catalogue had described it, and in this elevated state Craig and Delwin concluded there wasn't much difference between Americans and Canadians. They were all North Americans. The 49th parallel was just a line.

"I'm glad you feel that way, Craig, because you could do us a tremendous turn, I mean, it could change our lives, turn things around for Dianne and me."

"What's that?"

"Look, we've had a rough time here. Lost everything and almost lost our lives. If we were to go back into the States with you, as part of your party, would that be okay?"

"What do you mean back into the States. You're not Americans. You're from up here. You're Canadians."

"Yes, of course. No, we'd just go with you. Say we were returning to the States with you."

"That's illegal."

"Canadian customs will wave you on through and the Americans will say, "Where y'all from?" And you'll say, "Washington State," and they'll wave you through, too.

"It's not only illegal. It's unlikely. Impossible."

"But don't you see? That's just why it'll work. Because it's impossible. They'll be expecting Americans when you cross the border with Washington plates. And of course," he added, appealing to Craig's weakness, "when they see the Grand, the ski racks . . . well."

What absolute and complete lack of judgement now hurtled the Grand toward the border crossing! Craig worked the CD player. Susan sulked. In the rear seats, Delwin and Dianne held each other.

"I think we need more buoyancy in our ride," said Craig. "I'll adjust the suspension system module."

They were fourth at the border crossing, each second passing painfully slow.

"What'd I tell you?" said Delwin as the Grand inched steadily forward. "They're waving us on through."

Then the customs officer, having not stopped one of the three cars ahead, stepped in front of the Grand and raised his hand. Craig braked and the Grand stood still.

The customs officer was slowly walking around the rear of the GMA, so that he would be able to peer in from Susan's side when Susan suddenly remembered the garbage bags. She turned around and said to Dianne, "What did you say was in those bags?"

"Laundry," said Dianne. "Dirty laundry."

"I could scream," said Susan.

"Don't," said Craig, gripping the wheel. "Please don't scream."

The customs officer bent down and craned his neck to scan inside the Grand. "Anything to declare?"

In their minds they were going over what they would say if things suddenly and seriously went awry, as they now threatened to do.

Dianne's story implicated everyone but herself. Susan blamed it all on second-hand smoke. Craig's explanation focussed on helping his fellow man. Delwin didn't have a story and Dianne was whispering in his ear.

"We're almost there."

"Yes," Delwin thought to himself. "But where?"

He felt like he was going into four wheel drift again, only this time there wasn't even a steering wheel to hold onto.

Starfish and Seagulls

WAITING FOR THE FERRY in an acre of parked cars, Julia sits in the close air of a rented Camaro while tourists wander through heat waves rising off the asphalt. She rolls down the driver side window as a voice crackles through a loudspeaker. "Attention all Vancouver via Horseshoe Bay passengers. Our 3 PM departure for the mainland will be delayed. I repeat. The 3 PM sailing has been delayed."

The ferry had docked, the cars had unloaded, so why weren't they letting any cars on? And why didn't they announce how long the delay would be? Julia pulls the sun visor down and looks into its little mirror. What will happen to you now? she asks the miniature reflection, then shuts it, afraid to look. She flips the visor up, afraid to think, and squints into the glare, thinking about it anyway.

"Ever been to Vancouver Island?" Doctor Music, a.k.a. Bernie Sharpe, making his pitch, perched on the edge of his desk so he can look down the front of Julia's blouse. She considers kicking him between his legs dangling over the desk but instead says, "Just what is it I'm selling?"

"Music, Julia, music."

"Music of what, Bernie, the spheres? Mister Space Cadet, Mister, oh, I forgot, it's Doctor, isn't it, Doctor Music. There's music everywhere, Bernie. I mean, you can download it on your computer. That doesn't mean you can go around selling it."

"Sure, there's music everywhere, bad music. In a store, some whiney singer coming at you over the PA so loud and incessant there's nothing you can do but drop whatever you were thinking of buying and run. Bad music. Attacked again by bad music. Besieged by bad music. Bars, restaurants. It's everywhere. Held captive by bad music. Why Julia, I'll bet if I pick up this phone on my desk and dial a hotel or an airline, they'll put us on hold, and it'll be right in our ears, bad music."

He starts to dial.

"Hey, I believe you. What are you doing?"

He puts his hand over the mouthpiece. "Phoning my wife to tell her I won't be home for dinner. You and I have to talk about this."

To prove his point, Bernie takes her to a restaurant where the food is good and the music is bad.

"See, the first mistake, it's a vocal. With Doctor Music there's no vocals. Never again will you be attacked by inane lyrics. Strictly instrumental. Doctor Music gives you a tasteful format of light jazz that never offends. You plug it in and its on all day long. Unobtrusive unless you're listening for it, and if you are, it's great. Miles playing ballads. Bill Evans. Ben

Webster. All the standards but no vocals. Just the tunes."

"*Polka Dots & Moonbeams.*"

"What?"

"*Polka Dots & Moonbeams,*" the song. Can we have *Polka Dots & Moonbeams*?" She sets her drink down on the table.

"Sure, Julia."

"How about, "*It's Only A Paper Moon*?"

"Sure."

"And let's see, "*My Funny Valentine.*"

She tips her glass to drain it, holding it horizontal like a spy-glass, the ice cubes a lens through which she sees Bernie's distorted face, the little piece of shit who cheats on his wife.

"Which reminds me," she says, "what's that one you never hear nowadays? *It's the Talk of the Town.* Coleman Hawkins doing *It's the Talk of The Town* on that live set at the *Village Gate.* How wonderful! Bernie, it's a wonderful idea!"

She has now finished her third drink, and anything is possible.

"I want you to go over there and sign up the whole island. Rent a car. Start in Victoria and drive up island stopping at every store, restaurant, bar, even the hotels. You'll love it. A woman like you — hey, no problem. The whole island. You can do it, Julia."

"I don't know how you do it, Julia. Talking to complete and total strangers. Selling them something. It's so, I don't know, so sleazy."

Easy for her friend Claire to judge; Claire has money, Julia hasn't. Julia read somewhere, where was it, Jean Rhys, that was it, that a time comes in your life when, if you have any money, you can go one way, but if you have nothing at all — absolutely nothing at all — and nowhere to get any, well, then you go another way.

Which is how she got stuck travelling between two pieces of land separated by the straits. No, they did not want her songs. They did not want her music. In the end, all she wanted was a sale to cover her costs, but she didn't get it, not even enough to pay the car rental when she gets off the island, if she ever gets off the island. The car rental is on her credit card and when she returns the car and they make up the bill they'll discover the card is already maxed out.

But for now, no one is going anywhere. A collective road rage, an ugly energy palpable in the summer heat, simmers in the parking compound as drivers discover they are trapped. A man stalks toward the ticket booth, bangs his hand on the counter, rattling the glass, demanding answers. The woman inside shakes her head.

Sirens pierce the compound as a police car winds up the off-ramp and disappears in the dark hold of the ship. An ambulance follows.

The island gives Julia an acute sense of separation heightened now by the failure of the only means of getting off it, the ferry. But then, what's to return to? Nothing. She can't even pay for the car.

Something inside Julia is breaking, coming asunder, something to do with the straits, the passage, disconnecting from the mainland. She doesn't know. Doesn't understand. Later, she will blame it on the heat, but now she is not even thinking. She just knows she must get out of the chain-link parking compound.

She reaches into the back seat for her overnight bag and gets out of the car. Leave the keys, she decides. She drops them on the driver seat, and closes the door.

Walking away from the car, not her car, the car rental company's car, moving down the narrow space between the car rows, toward the distant sign mounted on a tin shed roof at the edge of the sea, *Muddy Water Tavern*, she can hear Claire's voice behind her.

"Stop Julia. It's Claire. You can't do this, you know. Just walk away from everything."

"Watch me, Claire! I can do anything I want!" Julia says aloud.

Witnesses would later recall a tall, middle-aged woman hurrying through the cramped space between the car rows, turning her body to avoid hitting a side mirror, and looking back, shouting to someone behind her.

"Shut up, Claire!"

But there is no one there.

The rooftop *Muddy Water Tavern* sign toward which Julia hurries does not refer to a blues singer but to the murky harbour sliding by under a bar built on pilings, and the character of the patrons within, who even this early in the afternoon fill "The Mud" to capacity.

Scene of constant transactions of a suspect nature, *Muddy Water Tavern* is a wholly owned subsidiary of the *Wild Waves Amazing Kingdom of the Sea*, a tourist attraction complete with its own golf course and gated community.

Frankie Cross, the manager of *Muddy Water*, has a lot to manage, especially today, for he alone knows the cause of the ferry's delay. His courier has been killed.

At crew change, a deckhand made his way out of the parking lot and over to *Muddy Water* to tell Frank that Charlie Burnette's van hadn't come off the ferry because Charlie Burnette couldn't be found.

Billy Fong's men must have got to him on the ferry. Well it wasn't the first time a drug war had been fought on the ferry. Fong's men used duct tape, the handyman's friend, and wire. Poor Charlie. Everyone knew he was carrying. A big ugly biker running a courier service out of his van who'd deliver anything for a price, drugs, money, bodies, dead or alive, and now Charlie was dead. He will have to be more careful who he hires as a courier, more discreet.

Frankie Cross has dismissed his bartender and taken over behind the bar because it gives him the best vantage point from which to keep his eye on the door. Any moment now, either Billy Fong, or the police, will walk through it.

The door is opening. A woman stands in the doorway, holding it open, a woman wearing a tailored black suit jacket and pants, holding the door open, trying to decide, he thinks, whether to come in.

When Julia opened the door a waft of beer and cigarette smoke stopped her and she stood staring into the smoke-filled din. She didn't need Claire to tell her this was not a good idea. Then, beyond the crowded bar, through its outer windows, she saw tables on a patio out over the pier. At last, she thought, and began making her way through the bar toward the patio.

The woman is walking toward him. Walking right through the bar toward him, some six feet away now, she stops and he studies her face. High cheekbones, a big nose and brown eyes and then she turns and walks through the bar and out the door onto the patio lounge. Gone. Still, she had taken his mind off Fong and the dead courier.

Julia orders a lime margarita, no salt, a good hot weather drink, but she will wait and see what the lime is like before she orders another, thinking already of the second drink before the first has arrived.

Thank you, thank you, ooh thank you! Her fingers close on the cool wet glass, raising it to her lips, holding it by the stem, like a chalice, her head uplifted to take in the sea before her, she sips her drink, listens to the gaiety of the summer crowd out on the water, and closing her eyes becomes for one small moment a girl without a care in the world, the girl on water skis.

Rented boats plane the surface of the sea towing bright bikini clad girls who bounce across the water

and whoop and shriek when their skis hit the wake. A
girl in a pink bikini lifts a hand from the tow bar to
wave at a sea plane descending overhead but at the
last moment loses her balance and in an instant is a
tangle of legs and arms thrashing in the water. The
girl's skis float loose on the chop and Julia watches her
bobbing head disappear and reappear as she treads
water.

The boat is circling back to pick her up, its engines
cut to an idle as two men lean over the bow, holding
their arms in the water for the girl to grasp.

No Julia, they will not circle back for you. You are
on your own, treading water, and you don't know how
long you can last.

"Another?" a voice behind her, the waiter reaching
over the table to take her empty glass, " . . . another
margarita?"

Julia nods a frantic assent, too frightened to speak.
The years have caught up to her, crowding in on her.
Where did they go, anyway? They slid by like the water
beneath the pier, until one day you are forty-five,
treading water and trying to keep from drowning.

You should have stuck with vitamins, Claire had
told her. Vitamins gave Julia a life after her kids had left
home, a reason to take care of herself, up in the morning
and on the road. Not door-to-door. No. The vitamin
company had her in stores, set up mid-aisle, dressed in
her navy pant suit, white shirt open, people gathering
around while she told them of the pill . . . its promise of
increased vitality, and renewed sexual energy, her
presence living proof of its power, rolling the big

orange oblong pill between her thumb and forefinger, holding it over a glass of water, then, at the exact moment, the precise moment that she alone could calculate, she would drop it into the glass and in an instant of effervescent fizz the capsule would dissolve and disappear.

A glass appears on the table. She stares at the margarita and hears laughter. The girl in the day-glo pink bikini is in the bar now.

Julia sucks lime juice and tequila through crushed ice, lets it lie cool on her throat, the ice melting, the delicious trickle of the liquor spreading through her body. Better, much better. She is developing a plan. She will simply walk into the bar and sell the manager the Doctor Music System.

Why not. She has all the paperwork in her bag. This is her last chance. Julia closes the door on the patio, stands just inside the bar and suddenly everything in it, even the table her hand grasps for support, seems slightly askew. Tilted. "You should have had something to eat instead of three drinks."

"Shut up, Claire."

The Doctor Music System representative walks steadily across the lounge and toward the bar, passing the table where the girl and her two rescuers are studying the menu.

"I'm hungry, Mike." One of the men slaps his menu down on the table. "By god, I'm hungry!"

The girl sits between two men in the middle of one of those horseshoe-shaped vinyl lounge seats, one arm around each of them, her bikini the same shade of day-glo pink as a salmon lure. The best thing she could have done was to lose her balance and fall in. Now they are buying her lunch.

"Well, let's get some wings."

"What kind of wings?"

"Hot wings."

Yes, that's what happened, isn't it Julia? You lost your balance and fell in, reaching out and grasping the bar stool, steadying herself, pushing herself up on the bar stool and into the glow of light from the bottles behind the bar.

"Is the owner or manager of this place around?"

"Why?"

"I'd like to speak to him."

"About?"

"About a music system that could really make a difference in a place like this."

"Oh yeah. In what way?"

"It would be different than this."

Overhead television screens beam their shifting images: a race car flips and skids down the track on its crumpled roof; on TNN, the Country Channel, Porter Wagoner and Little Jimmy Dickens are backstage between acts at the Grand Ole Opry.

"The music would define the place, the space. The music would create an energy and ambience that would make it the place to be. The Doctor Music System . . . "

"What kind of music we talking about?"

"Jazz. Mainstream."

"Jazz won't work here."

"How do you know if you've never tried it? Anyhow, I'd like to speak to the owner or manager."

"That's me, I'm the manager and I'm telling you it won't work here. Watch this. I want to show you something."

Frankie Cross points the remote at Porter Wagoner and Little Jimmy Dickens and in an instant they disappear as the remote rolls through the channels. "Here it is, Channel 133."

The screen is blank except for some titles over the bottom left corner. "What does that say?"

"Jazz Mainstream." She hears a guitar, a ballad, sad, wistful, melancholy. Grant Green. Sonny Clarke on piano.

"Why would we want your program when we already have jazz right here on the remote. Didn't your Doctor Music guy know about this? Hell, why buy his CD program when its right here on the dish. All the jazz anyone could want. Trouble is, no one wants it. They want this shit instead."

He aims the remote and Porter Wagoner and Little Jimmy Dickens reappear. Porter Wagoner is undoing the jacket of his glitter suit and getting friendly with Little Jimmy Dickens. They have, it seems, much to talk about.

Preempted by an American hillbilly and his midget sidekick. That stupid Bernie. Blink and the technology passes you by. You turn around and suddenly you're not onboard anymore. You're overboard and treading water.

"What's the matter? You don't look so well."

"This isn't fair. Look, this just isn't fair."

"What do you mean, isn't fair?"

"I came in here and asked to see the manager or the owner of this place."

"Yes. That's me. I'm the manager of *Muddy Water*."

"But you didn't tell me that. I didn't know you were the manager, so naturally I didn't give you a proper presentation of our Doctor Music System. It isn't fair because I didn't know I was talking to the manager."

"Maybe so. But like I said, everyone here already has Channel 133, which outdates your system, and anyhow, they don't use it because they don't want it."

It was *her* no one wanted. Her and her music. She used to turn to her piano, an old wooden frame upright grand that would envelop her small body, lost in the music, the old standards, lost inside the piano, the piano itself lost, gone now, like everything else. Sold to stay alive. So much gone and nothing left now but survival.

"It isn't fair," she says to herself, looking at the piano shoved against the wall of the bar, shut tight and neglected, bench withdrawn, lid down.

"I see you have a piano."

"Yeah but no one here plays it much."

"That's too bad. What kind of piano playing do you like, anyhow?"

"Loud, barrel-house piano. The players in those houses had to play loud just to be heard. Radiate with the eighty-eights."

"Piano playing isn't about loud. It's about space. Bill Evans. And touch. Red Garland."

He noticed her when she first came in and now this beautiful woman is talking to him about touch. A touch of class. Not like these bikini babes that pass through here every week. His boss will be pleased, and if he gets her a job, well . . . "Look, I'm sorry this music thing hasn't worked out for you but I might be able to help you get some work. Depends. You never know."

"Depends on what."

"What kind of work are you looking for?"

"What did you have in mind?"

"The owner of this place needs a courier."

"If he needs a courier why doesn't he hire a courier service?"

"Well it's not that simple. This place is part of a larger tourist centre, The *Wild Waves Amazing Kingdom of the Sea* but everyone around here just calls it *Wild Waves* and it includes the wharf, the marina, gas sales, the hotel, golf course, even the killer whale and his trainer out there in the pool, it's all part of *Wild Waves*, and it's all owned by one man, Argyle Roller. Wild huh? *Wild Waves*! See, there's a lot of important documents, paperwork, records, much of it of a confidential nature. For security reasons we prefer to manage our own transport, rather than rely on mail or a courier service."

Somewhere inside an alarm sounds but she pays it only token notice.

"Is it dangerous?"

"Just a ferry ride. There'll be someone to meet you at the other end. Are you interested?"

Claire would know what to do but Claire isn't here. What was it Jean Rhys had said? She has forgotten. Something to do with money.

"And the pay? What's the pay like?"

"Oh, *Wild Waves* is very generous. Are you interested?"

"Yes, I am interested."

"That's great. Listen, have you had lunch yet, because the oysters here are right out of the Straits of Georgia. Why don't I order you some while I phone my boss."

Julia nods a kind of assent, or is it surrender? It doesn't matter when you're hungry.

"I'll place your order and make a phone call about the courier job."

"If you don't mind I'll wait out on the patio."

A mistake, she realizes, as soon as she stands up. A bad case of the wobblies, like one of those flashlights you have to smack to get to work. Julia steadies herself, her hand on the bar stool, bracing herself to walk between the tables, across the room, and back out onto the patio.

In a few minutes lunch will come. Poached oysters topped with grated pecorino cheese and shredded prosciutto. "Another of the same, please waiter."

The afternoon wind is up. It bristles the hair on her arms and jostles the masts of the boats tied to the dock. The pilot of the float plane the girl on water skis had waved at has cut his engines and is letting the wind push the plane toward the wharf. Three men walk down the ramp, one backwards in front of a wheelbarrow loaded with what looks like firewood logs, the other grasping the wheelbarrow's handles, inching the load down the suspended ramp walkway that shakes in the wind that pushes the sea plane to the dock.

Another man follows down the ramp, all three of them on the float plane wharf now, two big men with hair cropped short on top, long at the neck, and a smaller man who seems to be in charge. They all wear identical aquamarine polo shirts, and although from the distance of the patio Julia cannot see the logo neatly embossed on their chest pockets, she knows it is the same logo as that on the bar manager's aquamarine shirt, *Wild Waves*. She watches them load flat slabs of flash frozen salmon from the wheelbarrow into the small plane. Even the waiter who brings her lunch wears an aquamarine *Wild Waves* polo shirt. "Should I run a tab?" he asks.

"The manager will take care of that," she says, firm, in control, but she is in over her head, treading water like the girl, only worse, deeper, more dangerous. Still, the wind is dying down. It is almost early evening, the cocktail hour.

Seagulls waddle along the dock, peck at garbage, clam shells, a salmon head, shitting a stream of grey-white slime as they go. One of them is struggling with a small starfish. A spiny purple leg pokes out of the gull's beak, the gull's oddly misshapen neck bulging with the bony starfish lodged within as the sucker tentacles on the underside of the starfish hold fast. The gull gulps but nothing happens, the starfish remains stuck in its neck. The gull gulps again, its effort weaker this time, more like a gasp as the starfish remains stuck in its throat, the gull choking on its own greed.

Seagulls shouldn't eat starfish, she thinks. As she looks down at her plate of oysters, she hears a voice from the table behind her.

"You see, Julia, this is what comes of not having a plan, of not thinking things out. You must always have a plan, and for emergency, a contingency plan."

"Shut up, Claire!" she says aloud, overwhelmed by the aroma of melted cheeses and Italian ham steaming off poached oysters. "Just shut up! All it means is seagulls shouldn't eat starfish. That's all!"

She is so very hungry. She lifts her fork toward the oysters but her hand trembles so badly she cannot hold it and the fork clatters onto the table. She holds her hand in front of her face and opens her trembling fingers to the evening light. If I had a cigarette, she decides, my hands would stop shaking. She looks down at the oysters and suddenly scoops one into her trembling hand, juice oozing between her fingers as she presses it into her mouth.

A real cigarette, Gaulloise or Gitane. If she just had one cigarette, her hands would stop shaking and she could play the piano in the bar.

In what now seems another world, the world outside the bar, a brief five minute walk from it, back at the terminal, the ferry is finally loading. Cars pass around the motionless Camaro, climb the ramp, and disappear one by one into the dark hold of the ship.

"This is an important announcement. Would the driver of a green Camaro, license plate AGA-328, please return to your vehicle. The ferry is now loading for Vancouver."

But the driver cannot be found.

HAVE YOU SEEN THE LIGHT, BROTHER?

I have seen the light. Its shining glory. Brother, I have seen the light.

No, not that light. This is the cold white light you see just before you die. There are witnesses and a survivor.

Larry was a roofer who scurried around on housetops faster than some people move with both feet on the ground, a little man living by the seat of his pants, middle-aged, balding, gray hair, and not much of it left, though he affected a slicked down ducktail because he had nerve and believed in God and thought it would cover the bald spots.

Larry knew God interceded on his behalf. Events were manipulated from above in Larry's favour. An obvious example that entered into his life on a daily basis was the weather. Larry wouldn't work wet roofs because they were dangerously slippery. You lost your footing and suddenly there you were, sliding down a high-pitched roof with nothing to stop you but the ground.

The construction crew would work two weeks in the rain and then on a bright sunny morning Larry's flatbed truck would appear loaded with bundles of red western cedar shakes. Larry's here and the sun is shining. The sun shone and Larry went to work. Everything he did was directed by God.

Only today it was raining and Larry wasn't working when he pulled up to the curb in front of his small rental, his flatbed truck loaded with resawns worth nothing now he'd lost the condo contract. He turned off the ignition, the stuttering afterburn of the engine fired on for several seconds while he glanced at his watch — 9:25 Sunday morning. Time to talk to the Big Guy, God's Man-Of-The-Hour (9:30-10:30), Wendell Wonderly, broadcasting live from Grace Cathedral in Akron, Ohio, to anywhere there was a television. Wherever Larry went, Wonderly was with him.

Larry got out of his truck, walked through a gate hanging off one hinge, and while he reached into his pocket for his door key, he glanced quickly at his tools piled in the narrow enclosed front porch. Like many people who live alone, Larry kept the television on, even when he wasn't home, so there would be a voice in his empty house when he entered it. Now, as he turned his key in the door, he could hear that voice on the other side.

"He has arrived. Oh, my friends, I can feel it. He is with us at this very moment in Grace Cathedral."

Larry immediately sat down in a chair in front of his television where the screen was filled with a shot from the heights of Grace Cathedral, not unlike God himself looking down on the congregation of thousands of standing, swaying, singing, believers. Then the camera switched to the owner of the voice, a huge man with jet black hair who wore a pale pink polyester suit.

"Open your hearts to Him," urged Wendell Wonderly, "for He is in our presence. Place your hand in mine. That's right. Right against the screen."

Larry pressed his hand against the screen, matching finger by finger over Wonderly's on-camera open palm.

"It feels so good, doesn't it? I have no power. I am only the channel through which He acts. We are connected now, all of us locked together in Holy Communion. Put your hand right there on the screen. Right there. That's right. We are connected. God, through me, is listening. And now while we are connected, locked together in communion, I want each and every one of you to give your own personal testimony. Tell God your hopes. Your desires. Your needs. God is listening."

In a rented clapboard, a man knelt before a television screen, its shifting light bouncing off the walls of the darkened room.

This was not the first time Larry had asked God for money. Larry waited until he was really desperate because you didn't want to trifle with the Big Guy. And you had to have your tithes paid up with Wendell Wonderly. There had to be a serious need. Larry needed three thousand dollars. The same light that bounced off the walls bathed Larry's face a glowing pink as he began to speak. The light emanated from the suit worn by God's Man Of The Hour, (9:30-10:30) Wendell Wonderly.

Larry told Wendell Wonderly and God how the contractor had advanced him money on materials. No. 1 hand-split western red cedar shakes, but Larry substituted resawns, and when the contractor found out, he wouldn't pay. He wanted his advance back or he would send his crew to collect.

A resawn, Larry explained to God and Wendell Wonderly, is a single hand-split cedar shake, its thickness cut in half from corner to corner to yield two shakes. A two for one split. Double your money.

"A win-win situation," Larry had enthused to the contractor, implying they could share in the booty.

But the contractor, as Larry was now explaining to God, hadn't seen it that way.

"Thin Larry. Too thin. Won't last. I have to live in this town. You charged me for full shakes, not resawns. Thin, thin, not fucking win-win. These resawns are worth exactly half what you charged me. You owe me three thousand dollars."

Not only did the contractor refuse to pay, he demanded the money back he advanced Larry for what he expected would be quality materials.

"When you look down on my roofs I know You are satisfied," Larry talking directly to God now. "God is satisfied with my roofs!"

Larry felt confident saying this because from the perspective of God looking down from heaven, God would see the hand split rough upper heavenward side of the shake, not the smooth under-cut of the resawn.

"Another thing, my roofs are ecologically responsible and environmentally friendly. Resawn means twice as many shakes cut from the same number of trees." Larry had become so involved in explaining the virtues of resawns to God he had forgotten to ask Him for money.

"And yet this man, this contractor . . . " the time of Larry's audience with God was almost over now . . . "Please God," he pleaded, "three thousand doll . . . "

But Testimony Time in Grace Cathedral had ended. There would be a brief message prerecorded in the Upper Room and then back to the live broadcast in Grace Cathedral and the healings.

"For those who can't join me in Grace Cathedral, this very special offer from the Upper Room.

"This is no ordinary edition of the New Testament."

Wendell Wonderly held what seemed a large black leather book, which he opened to reveal a carrying case loaded with cassettes.

Larry already had the tapes, so he was hardly listening, having only moments ago been in direct communication with God via Wendell Wonderly.

" . . . the actual recorded voice of Efrem Zimbalist Junior reading your favourite passages from the New Testament. To get these wonderful cassettes, complete with your very own simulated leather embossed carrying case, send one hundred and twenty-nine dollars to EFREM care of Wendell Wonderly, The Upper Room, Akron, Ohio. That address again: EFREM, care of Wendell Wonderly, The Upper Room, Akron, Ohio.

"Yes, friends," beamed Wendell Wonderly, unaffected by the telephone numbers crawling across his pink suit, "through the miracle of electronics the WORD has become the VOICE of EFREM ZIMBALIST JUNIOR."

When he was driving to work in his flatbed truck, Larry often played the tapes of Efrem Zimbalist Junior reading the New Testament but when he listened to the voice on the tapes, Larry couldn't help but remember Efrem Zimbalist Junior from the old FBI program on television. The program always ended with Efrem Zimbalist Junior in a helicopter flying over the criminals.

Crouched in the open hatch of the hovering helicopter, crease perfectly pressed in his shiny Sunset Boulevard slacks, Efrem Zimbalist Junior would shout down at the criminals through a megaphone, "This is the FBI!"

" ... order the New Testament tapes of Efrum Zimbalist Junior now and for a limited time only, choose from the exquisite Saint John The Baptist Steak Knife set, the embossed Noah's Ark Shower Curtain ... "

Messages were moving across the bottom of the screen in white letters ... SUPPLIES LIMITED . . . OFFER EXPIRES SOON ... VISA AND MASTER-CHARGE ORDERS ACCEPTED AT THIS TOLL FREE NUMBER ... 1-800-EFREM.

Then the camera was live in Grace Cathedral and it was time for the healings. Wendell Wonderly healed people and broadcast the healings live to the world.

People came to be healed and people came to witness the healings.

"State your name, and the nature of your affliction."

Two assistants stood behind the afflicted to catch them as they fell backward from the force in Wonderly's hands.

Larry hardly noticed, preoccupied as he was with his own problems. Even though he had not quite finished putting the *and* on three thousand, Larry believed God would help him. It was only a matter of time.

A week went by and nothing. Larry was now threatened with eviction. He paced in and out of the clapboard rental, the door open onto the front porch, back and forth between the kitchen, the living room, and out onto the porch, all the while talking frantically to God and Reverend Wendell Wonderly.

"You must . . . you must . . . " Larry stepped out onto the porch shouting, arms waving.

On the sidewalk, four Indians stopped to stare. The Indians made Larry uncomfortable and now that he was broke and out of work their presence was a constant reminder of his reduced circumstances. The police had the right idea. Their solution was as old as the frontier, the "get out of town" solution. The police were known to drive the Indians out of town in the back of their patrol cars and drop them off in the countryside. All his life Larry had worked hard and what did he have to show for it? God might as well have made him an Indian.

"What the hell are you staring at?" he yelled.

The Indians didn't answer, instead talking to each other in Cree, and turning, pushed their shopping cart down the sidewalk.

One of them was walking on either side of the cart because the front right wheel was bent and as they pushed the cart it veered to the right. The bottles and cans in the basket jiggled and vibrated and under the rattle of the moving cart the bent wheel *kachunkachunk*ed down the sidewalk, the sound fading down the street as Larry watched the Indians try to direct the cart's course.

He turned to walk back into the house and stopped to stare at the collection of tools and supplies piled on his porch; a compressor, roofing hammer, ladder, tarps, the chainsaw. None of it was any good to him now that he had no work.

And why had he hauled a chainsaw onto the prairies where there were no trees to cut anyway? Because he couldn't part with it, a Stihl 066 with a decompression chamber so you didn't tear your arm off starting it, a saw worth at least three thousand dollars new, one of the few things Larry had ever bought new. He remembered taking it out of the box and reading the owner's manual. The section on kickback read like a physics text stating a basic law of the universe: for every action there is an equal and opposite reaction.

Kickback occurs when the upper quadrant of the bar nose contacts a solid object or is pinched. The reaction of the cutting force of the chain causes a rotational force on the chainsaw in the direction opposite to the chain movement. This may fling the bar up and back in an uncontrolled arc mainly in the plane of the bar. Under some cutting circumstances, the bar moves towards the operator, who may suffer severe or fatal injury.

Well, he wouldn't have to worry about kickback anymore because he was going to sell the saw. He picked it up off the porch, carried it out to his truck, slammed the cab door shut, and turned the key.

The battery was dead. Contacts. He got out, lifted the hood, moved the battery cables, dropped the hood, got back in the truck cab and it started first crank. Contacts, gunning the engine, contacts every time.

Larry did not have to drive far to find a pawnshop. He already knew he wouldn't get enough for the chainsaw to clear himself with the contractor and pay his rent. God and Wendell Wonderly would take care of the shortfall. He had not lost faith, merely modified it.

Lo-Budget Pawn & 2nd Hand
Once In A Lifetime Bargains

The man in the pawnshop was thin, caved in on himself, couldn't lift his chin off his sunken chest to look at Larry when he spoke to him, so he looked at him by rolling his eyes upward.

"Eight hundred dollars. Best I can do."

"It's worth more than that."

"Not here it isn't. Take it, or leave it. You want the eight hundred or not?"

"I'll take it."

"There's no record," he said, chin on his chest, eyes on the bills, counting out eight hundred dollars.

"What?"

"No record," looking right at Larry now with his eyes rolled upward, his chin still on his chest. "I don't keep records. It's better for me and it means you can claim it."

"Claim it?"

"Claim the insurance. Report the saw stolen. That way you get the money from selling it, and the money from the insurance. It's a win-win situation."

It was an expression Larry was familiar with. "Why don't you keep records?" he asked.

This time he didn't bother to raise his eyes to Larry when he answered. "Most of the stuff in my shop is stolen."

"I'll be back with more tools!" Larry shouted. "Thank you, Jesus! Thank you, Wendell Wonderly! Thank you, God!"

Larry sold everything, reported it stolen, and filed an insurance claim.

"Happens all the time," the officer told him. "Break-ins. There's just one thing I don't understand," said the policeman, staring at his notes.

Larry had told the officer his tools were padlocked in the spare bedroom and he'd come home to find the front door ajar, the lock broken, and the tools missing. He said the tools were locked in the bedroom because the insurance wouldn't cover theft of tools left on his porch.

"Just one thing."

"What's that?"

"What were you doing with a chainsaw way out here on the prairies where there's no trees to cut?"

"I loved that chainsaw," choked Larry. "Couldn't bear to part with it when I left the coast, so I brought it with me. Now it's gone, stolen."

"It doesn't get much lower than stealing a man's tools," commiserated the police officer, though to himself he was wondering how anyone could love a chainsaw.

"Have you any idea," he said, shutting his notebook, "who might have done this?"

"Not really."

"No one you saw who acted suspicious, out of place?"

"Well," began Larry, trying to help. "There were some Indians."

"Indians?" said the police officer, opening his notebook again. "What about the Indians?"

"Four of them."

Larry offered what details he could: the wonky wheel of the shopping cart, the clatter of the bottles, a baseball cap on backwards, not much to go on really, but who knew?

With the money from the sale of his tools to the pawnshop, he paid the rent, bought himself a small used car, and settled into winter while he waited for the insurance claim to come through.

When the police picked up Natives they questioned them about Larry's chainsaw.

"Are you crazy?" one young man demanded. "What would I do with a chainsaw when there are no trees to cut?"

Rumour had it that if the Indians became unruly, obnoxious, or in any way disagreeable with the officers, they drove them out of town.

It was called the "Midnight Run" and the route was always the same. Natives were placed in a patrol car and driven on the road that followed the river out of town, past the scrubby wasteland beyond the city dump, past the power station, and dropped off in an adjoining field.

In his weekly newspaper column, a city police constable who thought himself something of a writer, described the "Midnight Run" for the amusement of his readers. In the officer's fictionalized account, the policemen picked up a beligerent drunk who demanded to be taken to the highest power in the land. The officers obliged by driving him out of the city and abandoning him at the power station.

It was, after all, only a fictionalized account. The drunk was never identified as an Indian, but his demand to be taken to "the highest power in the land" was a backhanded reference to nineteenth century treaty negotiations, when Native leaders asked to meet with the highest power in the land, thus the power station as the place of abandonment. The truth was that in the dead of winter, when temperatures dropped to -30, the police drove Indians out of town and abandoned them. A member of the provincial Legislature, out for her morning run, found the partially frozen body of a young Indian man, and four days later, railway workers found the frozen body of another Indian in a field near the power station.

Larry was as preoccupied as ever with the problem of cash flow. The money from the pawnshop sale had run out, the insurance claim hadn't paid yet, and he was drinking.

The thing about Larry's drinking was that it didn't show. You didn't notice it. Larry could still see the picture, it was just a little blurred at the edges of the screen.

A television newscaster wearing a parka stood in front of the power station where the bodies had been found, his freezing breath fogging into the microphone as he described how the Indians had died of hypothermia. The same night the first man disappeared, another Native lived through the experience. He claimed he was picked up by the police, handcuffed and driven out to a field 100 yards from the power station, before being kicked out of the car. Dressed in only a jean jacket, with no hat or gloves, the Indian ran to the power station, where he banged on the door for 10 minutes before a night watchman let him in. He was laying charges against the police.

All this meant nothing to Larry, who had fallen asleep in his chair. The last words he heard before he slipped into sleep was the newscaster describing the death of the Indians. Not only was Larry asleep, he was now in the throes of a deep dream, a revelation, a recurring nightmare from which he would wake, but which would never go away, recurring again not identically, but each time developing some horrible new detail.

Larry is running through a field of dry, fall wheat, the husks flicking against his face and body, the distant drone of aircraft above. Directly overhead now, tracking him, a helicopter hovers, the thrashing beat of its wings flattening the wheat to the ground in a widening circle as it descends upon him. Larry lies flat on the ground.

Larry cannot make out the figure standing in the darkened interior of the open helicopter hatch door. Is it God . . . Wendell Wonderly . . . Efrem Zimbalist Junior? Whoever it is, he is wearing a well-cut suit that fits snugly across his broad shoulders. The man is climbing down from the helicopter hatch. The man carries something that looks much like a violin case, but longer and bulkier, made of moulded grey plastic of the type used on power tool cases. The man turns his back to Larry, places the case on a table, and flips open the clasps with his thumbs.

Wait a minute. How did a table get out in the middle of a wheat field? This whole thing has been prearranged. God must be sending him a profound message. But what is it? Larry wonders, staring at the twin-plaited black braids tapering to nothing on the man's massive back. The man bends forward, reaches into the case, and turns to face Larry.

The biggest Indian Larry has ever seen yanks on the starter rope of a Stihl O66, and with only one pull, the saw springs to life, roaring; its razor-sharp teeth zipping around the bar so fast they are just a blur of blue glinting steel.

"I've come to return your chainsaw!" The Indian waves the saw over his head, revving the engine, gunning it.

"Stop Lawrence!" calls the Indian. "I've come to return your chainsaw!"

And always, it is the sound, the roar of the chainsaw alive and running in the big man's hands that wakes him. Again and again he wakes from the same dream. The Indian waving the chainsaw over his head, the chainsaw running, Larry running.

As surely as Larry had believed God would intercede on his behalf, he now believed God was sending him a profound message. But what? What did it mean? It was driving him mad. The nightmares. The waking noise of the chainsaw.

He couldn't sleep so he drank to pass out and still the roar of the chainsaw woke him, and in the end, broke him. A roofer afraid of heights, you'd see him on a Sunday morning standing at the back of some four square gospel country church trembling, and then suddenly, he'd burst through the congregation and begin to tell his story.

His vision. His revelation.

In the churches where Larry testified, there was much discussion over the meaning of the apparition. Larry's vision was studied the way theologians study scripture.

Was the huge Indian wielding the chainsaw the Antichrist or an avenging God?

Larry wrote to Wendell Wonderly and described his vision.

What did it mean? And why does the apparition call me by my formal name, Lawrence. I await your enlightenment. L. Doyle.

Unfortunately, the man of synthetic cloth never read Larry's letter. The computer that processed all incoming mail at Words of Wonder headquarters in Akron, Ohio, dutifully noted Larry was not enclosing $129.00 for the Efrem Zimbalist Junior New Testament tapes, not ordering the End of the World Lawn Furniture that doesn't melt in the heat, and so it locked Larry's address inside a silicon memory chip, whereupon the Words of Wonder computer began to send a constant flow of mail advertising Reverend Wendell Wonderly's religious writings.

Once a week a small reply card advertising the reverend's religious literature appeared in Larry's mail. One featured a photograph of the Tower of London, Execution Block and Axe. "The axe has been in the tower since 1236. The block is that on which Lord Lovat was executed." Larry looked at the axe and it reminded him of the Indian in his vision wielding the chainsaw. He gulped down his drink, flipped the card over, and read the other side.

HOW TO SPEED READ THE BIBLE IN TIMES OF CRISIS. (19 pages) An inspirational pamphlet by the Reverend Wendell Wonderly. Another dynamic contribution to the salvation of the human race . . . only $25.95. Words of Wonder publications. Akron, Ohio.

Larry poured himself a drink and puzzled over another of the reverend's mad missives that arrived in the mail each week.

ANGST FOR THE MEMORIES (72 pages 3 photographs 1 map) Reverend Wendell Wonderly's own account of his early years as a bible salesperson in Moose Jaw before he underwent his personal conversion to the living reality of Jesus Christ.

" . . . a searing indictment of self-appointed religious software peddlers everywhere who know not what they do."

— *Bible Times Magazine*

" . . . absolutely terrific! A brutally frank and touching testament — a reaching out — displays deep humility and searching self-awareness . . . highly recommended!"

— *Christian Life Today*

A WARNING . . . AND A BEACON . . . FOR
SEEKERS EVERYWHERE.
Yours for $24.95 from Words of Wonder, Akron, Ohio.

Larry poured himself another drink, his third, one for each of the three communications he had received from Wendell Wonderly, and read the latest arrival in the mail.

WOULDN'T IT BE WONDERLY! At last! The long-awaited third volume of the autobiography of the Rev. Wendell G. Wonderly — as told in his own words to Rachael Chateaubriand-Wonderly — featuring the unravelling of the knot of mysteries and the conundrum surrounding the man of God's ancestral, cultural, and spiritual origins.

Part III in which we meet the spiritual teachers who guided young Wonderly's footsteps onto the humble path of miracles he treads today. $34.95 at religious bookstores everywhere!

Where was the enlightenment? The light? The salvation?

He finished his drink and staggered out of his house onto the street. What if the same demented brain that produced the messages he received in the mail was the God he had hoped and prayed would intercede on his behalf? No wonder everything had gone so wrong since he lost the condo contract. God was a joker who left his calling card in the mail and manipulated events to suit his own amusement. If this was so, he was truly fucked. If this was so, everyone was . . .

"Doomed!" Larry suddenly shouted. "We're all doomed!"

People parted on either side to make way for the short middle-aged man who thrust his arms in the air and staggered toward them. It was too cold to stop or even slow down and they hurried on by.

"Will you look at that."

Buddy Sykes had his patrol car barely moving, crawling alongside the curb so that he and his partner, Sid Fletcher, could reach into the box full of Tim Hortons on the front seat between them and slowly eat the night away in the comfort of their patrol car.

"I'd rather not," said Buddy, who could already see it was trouble.

Half a block ahead, a man stumbled down the sidewalk, shouting warnings of imminent ruin at every passerby.

"Doomed! It's in the scriptures! The New Testament! Efrem Zimbalist Junior!"

Inside the patrol car, Buddy Sykes and his young partner Sid Fletcher couldn't hear the words Larry was shouting.

"We've got to do something. He's accosting people."

"Okay. Look, I'll accelerate, turn in on the curb, drive up onto the sidewalk, and we'll cut him off. That way, with the car up on the sidewalk, we'll be out of the car an absolute minimum amount of time because, I'm telling you, it's cold out there. If he gives us trouble we can drop him off at the power station."

"I don't think he's Indian," said Fletcher, now that they were closer and he could see Larry's face.

"Hell," laughed Sykes, "we don't discriminate!" He had one foot poised on the brake, the other on the gas, because he knew that was the only way he could make his manoeuvre work.

Sykes gunned the engine, they bounced up over the curb, and he hit the brakes.

As if it had dropped suddenly out of space, the patrol car straddled the sidewalk in front of Larry, the throbbing strobe of its red dome light flashing in his face.

"Thank God you're here!" said Larry to the two policemen who burst from the front seat of the patrol car.

There was one on either side of him now, walking him to the patrol car, pushing his head down as they shoved him into the back seat. They got in the front seat and turned to face him through the wire mesh barrier.

"Well," said Sykes, "what's this all about?"

Larry explained loudly. The lost condo contract. Wendell Wonderly. The vision of the chainsaw and the Indian. Efrem Zimbalist Junior, even the FBI. And there was more.

Sykes already had the car in gear.

"We're doomed!" Harry shouted through the wire cage at the officers. "Doomed!"

The crazies were the worst, thought Sykes, driving south along the road that follows the river out of town. You never knew what they were going to do next. Fletcher had been on the force just two weeks, fresh out of a junior college police program and was trying to block out the ravings from the man in the back seat by staring out the passenger side window when the last street light slid by. They had just passed the city dump. He knew where Sykes was driving, and he knew nothing could have prepared him for this night.

Tires crunched on the packed snow as Sykes drove through an open gate and into the centre of a snow-covered field enclosed in barbed wire. Sykes liked to watch in the rear-view mirror for the look on their face when they realized they were not being driven home, or, indeed, even to jail, but for a ride in the country. That always occurred either before or just after they passed the last street light; there would be this uneasy silence in the back seat and Sykes would watch the fear in the man's face, but this guy just kept on ranting.

"Read the scriptures!" shouted Larry. "The New Testament. Efrem Zimbalist Junior. The FBI!"

"The FBI huh?" Well, listen Mr. FBI, we'll all get out of this car now, you, me and my partner here, and we'll walk out here in this field, and you can explain it all to us again."

One minute all three were standing in the field, and the next, the two police officers had jumped back in their car and were driving away.

"See," Sykes said, and he did a little S-shaped skid on the snow as the car sped out of the field, "the secret is to get them in and out of the car quick so they don't have time to react, so they don't know what's happening. This guy didn't have a clue. He's got it now though," said Sykes, hungrily watching the rear-view mirror where a man was waving his arms and jumping up and down.

"He's really got it now," he said, watching the frantic man disappear into a dot inside the mirror.

When Larry stopped waving and jumping up and down, the cold penetrated to his core. He had to keep moving, but in which direction? There was nothing but flat, open prairie and in the distance, a mile away, the lights of a building, three huge smokestacks, civilization.

Larry was having difficulty walking, a stiffness in his muscles and a trembling in his left leg causing him to stagger. And yet, true to the symptoms of the first stages of hypothermia, he was unaware of his jerky, uncoordinated movement.

In the distance the power station hummed on, plumes of black smoke pouring from three smokestacks, a light in every window of the chain-linked facility. Larry stumbled toward that light, but what he actually saw now that hypothermia hampered his vision, was uncertain.

As in all his trials, he was talking to his God, calling out His name in his hour of need.

"Why me? What have I done to deserve this?"

And as if in answer, the light that emanated from within the power station cast its cold truth upon the snow. Had he not falsely accused the Indians of stealing? Had he not questioned God's will, saying God might as well have made him an Indian? And had he not approved of the police treatment of the Indians?

Beyond the city dump, on a night so cold wild dogs and coyotes would not move, Larry stumbled and fell in the snow.

On the television the healings continued.
State your name and the nature of your affliction.

Unravelling

WE LOADED UP THE CAR and drove right down into New Orleans. As we were crossing Lake Pontchartrain Bridge it was raining so hard that we couldn't see to drive. The wipers on my Chrysler were not working, so we took coat hangers and tied them to the blades and worked them by hand so that the driver could see the road. We didn't want to stop because we were afraid we would miss the session next morning.

— Richard Penniman

"Did you see that old man climb out of the ditch back there?"

"No."

"No wonder, the speed we're travelling."

"You got a problem with my driving, you can drive."

She punched the eject button on the stereo and a mess of unravelled cassette tape landed in her lap.

"This tape's ruined."

"Throw it out the window, then."

THWAP! The car's wind thrust hit Russell full force and knocked him to the ground. His glasses! Hands scrambling blindly among candy wrappers, cans and cardboard, frantically searching the roadside debris, a momentary difficulty, groping in society's discarded refuse, of which he himself was a part, until he found them and placed the taped cracked lenses on his weathered face in time to see the car disappear into a distant speck down the highway. And just as it did, something was thrown from its window.

"This Bud's for you!" Russell joked bitterly to himself, thinking the thing tossed from the speeding car was another can. It tumbled to the pavement and glinted in the sun.

Scouring the windblown corridor between the fence and highway, the old man bent to pick a squashed beer can out of the ditch and dropping it in his sack, focussed on the shiny object ahead.

The wind force of another car hit his back but this time Russell heard it coming. He'd turned off his radio, a crude ghetto blaster rescued from a garbage can, its plastic encased speakers silent now, the only sound the cans rattling in his sack, the swish of the passing car, the lift and flutter of cardboard and paper litter in the passing wind gust, and something else, something he was noticing everywhere.

In the traffic islands, wrapped around telephone poles, fenceposts, road signs, looped ribbons of brown acetate tape unravelling at the side of the highway. Caught on the bottom and middle strand of wire fences, brown shiny ribbons streamed in the sun, fragments of music silenced forever.

The car sped into the horizon. He too once had a life and hurtled from point to point in it. He had driven across the country six times, until, in the end, even the cities were a kind of journeying to the highway, home a black ribbon of asphalt, always just ahead, that he never arrived at. Long after he had stopped driving, after he had lost everything, his home, his marriage, even his identity, Russell still believed he had to keep moving, that if he stopped, he would die, here, at the side of the highway.

Russell Finch had fallen through every crack in the system until now, at the end of the century, fence wire defined his world, the twenty-foot roadside margin between the edge of the highway pavement and the farm fences. Not another human in sight and he liked it that way. People wanted him to keep his distance. Visualize him in their space no longer than it takes to open a disposal receptacle, quickly forage through it, and move to the next one, or down the highway to the next discarded aluminum can, as he was doing now. If he kept moving, he didn't threaten anyone because they didn't perceive him as existing in their world. It was the chance encounters he had to avoid; an alleyway, a bus in West Vancouver.

"Some shitload of cans," said the driver, handing Russell a transfer when he got on in West Vancouver packing two garbage bags bulging with cans, one over each shoulder. As his total bulk was more than three people, the only place Russell could sit was in one of those long seats that ran the length of the window at the front of the bus. The seats that face each other across the aisle and the one across from him were empty when he sat down. Then at Park Royal, the last stop before crossing the Lions Gate bridge into the city, an old woman slowly ascended the step well and made her way up the aisle, the driver watching in his rear-view mirror, not pulling out from the curb until she was seated directly opposite.

Forced to stare into each other's faces three feet across the aisle, the bejewelled wrinkled matron of West Vancouver practiced a kind of concentrated myopia that allowed her to look right through Russell, to neither see nor acknowledge the homeless man who sat across from her.

She rang the bell just before Georgia and Burrard but did not begin to make her way from her seat until the driver pulled to the curb and came to a complete stop. They could wait, and wait they would, everyone on the bus watching as she inched forward on her cane, and then, just before she descended the step well, she leaned over to tell the driver something, then stepped down to the unfolding doors: tea at the *Hotel Vancouver* and shopping at *Chapmans*.

The driver moved back out into the traffic, glanced up at Russell in the rear-view mirror, and snapped, "This next stop is where you get off."

The doors parted and he stepped from the passenger well of the bus and onto the street, miles from the recycling centre. He would never get there before it closed. Stuck with two bulging bags of aluminum cans just because an old lady had complained to the bus driver.

This is where you get off. Seventy-nine-years-old and so frail the wind from a passing car had knocked him off the side of the road and into a drainage ditch. And yet, to his surprise, waking this morning in the cold first light to find himself alive and fending for another day, even if he hadn't known where he was.

Russell had grown up in a time when each small town had its own individual identity but now all the towns looked the same, especially from the highway. The same strip mall was duplicated sixty kilometres further down the road. No wonder he hadn't known where he was this morning. Not that you slept in, not in culverts, boxcars, and dumpsters. No, you did not sleep in, not in a dumpster.

Five in the morning, Russell climbing out of a dumpster, not garbage, your worship, no garbage in that dumpster, just flattened cardboard boxes and Styrofoam behind some computer store, trying to get a grip to climb its shiny steel inside walls, one hand pushing up on the heavy iron hatch, other hand over the outside, crouched tottering on the high metal rim, Russell jumped back into the alley, and damn near jumped on top of this guy. Who would expect anyone else in an alleyway at 5 AM? It was still dark, your honour. Landed right in front of him and he freaked. Came apart. Screaming nuts. Stood there yelling at the top of his lungs like he'd been attacked. Police! Help! Police!

Sixty days for assault. A hard cold winter of bus stations, subway entrances, dumpsters, doorways, and finally, jail.

But it was summer now and Russell was free to collect his cans, still eyeing the one ahead, closer now. He thought of them recycled as mobile homes. He had lived in such a place, a mobile home park, the aluminum twilight zone, he called it.

On this stretch of highway the only music was country so having the radio turned off was a blessing. Better silence than some sad-ass hillbilly shit. In the silence, Russell heard the music that was in him, the music nothing could turn off. Even now, as he dragged his sack down the windblown corridor to the next beer can, snatches of melody, song, lyric, entire solos, ran, through his head.

He was now close enough to see that the glinting object was just more cassette tape. Though it shone in the sun like a can, up close there was no resemblance.

Disappointed, too tired to go on, Russell collapsed into the dried out drainage ditch, the cassette still in his hand, tape looped around his fingers. And as he idly turned one finger in the sprocket, the notion formed in his mind that if he could get the cassette tape untangled and rewound intact, he might play it on his machine.

His trembling index finger rewound the cassette sprocket while his left hand, unravelling the tangled tape, shook with excitement. It was untitled; somebody had taken the time and trouble to record some music but not label it.

Who and what would Russell hear? Miles brooding over *My Funny Valentine*, the big block chords of Red

Garland, Ben breathing into his tenor, or, cruelest of all, silence, nothing but the dead hiss of tape.

In Montreal, Russell had a friend who measured his mortality by the state of health of his fellow musicians.

"Maynard looks good tonight," he'd say, or, "Maynard looks really bad tonight."

Russell now realized every musician he had been hearing in his mind was dead. Time running out, unravelling, the tape rewound now, he flipped open the cassette compartment, placed the cassette inside and closed it. Time to hit PLAY.

If, in fact, the cassette player would work. His finger pressed the PLAY button. He peered into the scratched plastic viewing plate and watched the tiny cassette sprocket jerk to life. Then, the opening hiss of tape burst into a manic voice bellowing nonsensical lyrics:

A WOP BOP ALU BOP A WOP BAM BOOM!

He had seen Little Richard on his first road tour in 1956 and like most whites who witnessed the birth of the new music, Russell had been caught completely unaware. Listening to his band, the Upsetters, warm up the small-town audience playing an hour of solid black rhythm and blues had been a revelation. Alto, tenor, and baritone saxes honked, swooped, and bopped, Fender guitars and drums drove the backbeat, and Little Richard himself, sweating in his baggy suit, pummelled the piano with both hands and his right foot.

It sounded as fresh and outrageous now as it did then, and listening to the music now, a part of Russell was no longer dying at the side of the road, but was back on the island in Nanaimo where he had first heard that music, back before everything had started to go wrong, the timeless music taking him outside time.

When the music ended, it was followed by polite bemused applause that made him realise he was listening to a live recording. A voice began speaking in rapid fire staccato, jamming song titles together.

LongTallSallyTuttiFruitiRipItUpTheGirlCan'tHelpItShe's GotIt! OW! OW! OW! Wherever you've been, I've gone. I'm back. I am the only thing left. I am the originator, the architect, the one who started all of it!

Out of a cassette discarded on the side of the highway, at the end of the twentieth century, the Georgia Peach himself was unravelling one last time. Very soon, the old man knew, the batteries would be dead, but it didn't matter. He was lost in the burnt out silicon memory chip of time, and Little Richard was broadcasting on the airwaves of his mind.

First Night Out

THEY WERE SITTING IN HIS FRIEND'S KITCHEN drinking coffee, old schoolmates from the island, though that was all they had in common now. Danny's friend had attained the gentility of Point Grey, the university district, tree-lined boulevards and Volvos. But things had not gone well for Danny, and he was thankful just to have a roof over his head. Though, after staying for two weeks, he knew he had outworn his welcome. Time to ship out, he thought.

"Not just any boat," he explained, watching his friend grow impatient, wondering how long he was going to stay. "It has to be the right boat."

In the morning he caught a Number 10 Cross Town to the Seaman's Hall in the east end of the city to check the employment board. As the bus moved slowly down Hastings, he remembered, working as a copy boy at the *Vancouver Province* when it was the city's morning newspaper. They put the last edition to bed at midnight, and then, the night's work done, they would walk out of the building onto Hastings, the street rough but alive and vital. *The Balmoral*, where his uncle stayed when he came out of the camps, The *Smiling Buddha*, that bottle club around the corner on Main, *The New Delhi*, and the old Swede bent over the steaming clams in *Joey's*, *The Ho Inn*, the *Orange Door*, *Murray Goldman's* where he bought his clothes, *Woodwards*, and all the other shops and joints, gone now, the three blocks beginning at the old *Province* building, east across Main, taken over by junkies. Out Danny's bus window wasted and disheveled forms huddled and shuffled in the shadows of the entrances and alcoves to the boarded up abandoned buildings, shifting, scratching, waiting for a fix. It was their street now and no one else went there.

Danny got out at Hastings and Victoria and walked to the Seaman's Hall. It was filled with young men who would work any boat they could get, even the garbage barges that serviced the freighters anchored in the harbour, put a little time in and get some seniority. They looked up from their coffee and magazines, watching him study the board.

Danny Stone, member of the Seaman's Union Local, 400, searched three rows of cards, each card stating a berth and position on a boat. Then he reached out and removed one from the board and read it a second time.

Etta Mae
cook/deckhand
Wednesday 12:01 a.m.

Etta Mae . . . Etta Mae . . . Rita Mae . . . Jenny Mae, sister ships; he knew that boat, the only survivor of the three, the *Etta Mae* was one of the last of the wooden hull tugs still working the coast. Oh yes, he remembered the *Etta Mae*, a one hundred and twenty foot towboat with long low lines and a big single screw prop driven by a 1,250 horse power Superior diesel.

"I'll take it," he said, handing in the card.

The dispatcher never tried to discourage Danny's hope of getting on a boat, but when he looked at the card and saw it was the *Etta Mae*, he said, "You know, it's not a towboat, oldtimer. Hasn't been for years. They converted it to a fish-packer."

"So?"

"Well, it's not the same. It's not the same at all."

"But the boat is," replied Danny. "The boat's the same."

He stood at the end of the pier watching his phantom ship come out of the night toward him. Did he see it in his mind a split second before its actual appearance, a speck on the night's water slowly enlarging into the profile of its classic lines? A relic from another age, the curl of its wake white and phosphorescent against the black planking of its hull, the *Etta Mae* cut through the night water. The margin of white water between the boat and pier closed, the boat churning full astern now, but still moving irrevocably forward to the dock and hitting it hard, shaking the wharf Danny hurried down until he reached midship, the deck of the boat level with the dock, he jumped onboard.

The boat pulled back from the dock and he set his bag down in a nest of uncoiled rope and tried to find his sea legs. He cleared a path on the littered deck, working his way down the starboard and then up the port side of the boat. As he bent to coil the lines, each in its distinct place, bow lines, spring lines, stern lines, he was aware they were watching him from above, faces he could not see behind the darkened wheelhouse glass.

In the wheelhouse, Freddie Baker's sister was unpacking supplies while Freddie maneouvred the big boat back from the dock. His partner, Lyle Thomas, sat in the chair next to Freddie at the wheel and looked down at Danny on the deck below.

"I don't like the way that boy moves," he said.

"What's wrong with him?" demanded Freddie. "He showed up, didn't he?"

"He moves slow, as if he's doing this for the first time, or maybe trying to remember it from some other time, a long time ago. I tell you, it's dangerous. Not just for him. For all of us. For Christ sake! Look at him! He walks funny!"

"You'd walk funny too, if you were dodging a coffin." Freddie spun the wheel and watched the moving lights in the harbour.

"That boy, as you call him, is on the wrong side of sixty. If you weren't almost the same age, you'd see that yourself. An old guy like that, he'll never figure us out. He's perfect. Besides, he makes us legal. Now Lyle, I hope we're on course about this. We're both looking at the same chart, aren't we? The same water? Because in a minute he'll be up here in the wheelhouse to meet the happy crew. That's us, Lyle, and don't you forget it. This is my show, my crew."

"That may be," said the woman. "But it's my money. Everything I've got's tied up in this. So Lyle, it's like Freddie says, on course. There's no room for mistakes here."

Danny entered through the galley, made his way up a narrow passage filled with the roar and clatter of the diesel, knocked on a panel door, and stepping inside adjusted his eyes to the darkness of the wheelhouse.

In the glow of instrumentation the silhouette of a figure stood grasping the wheel, steadying the *Etta Mae* on course. Next to him a short bulky man was turning to face him.

"Sorry about not docking just now when we picked you up. Name's Thomas. Lyle Thomas. This's Marlene and Freddie Baker at the wheel. You're Danny Stone, right?"

The green line on the radar screen made its sweep, momentarily illuminating Thomas's face and a glimpse of a short, muscular man who looked like he laboured outdoors. On the port side a woman was kneeling over some boxes, unpacking. The man at the wheel did not turn toward him.

This time Danny waited for the sweep of the radar and when it came round he saw a rifle of some kind, butt on the deck, barrel angled at the port side, the woman kneeling over the boxes, talking to herself.

"My life consists of packing and unpacking. I unpack, pack up again, move somewhere else, unpack . . . "

"Shut up, Marlene!" said Freddie Baker. "If you would label the boxes, you wouldn't go through this shit every time we ship out, and I wouldn't have to listen to you when I'm trying to concentrate on getting us under this bridge."

They were approaching the Lions Gate Bridge and the channel it spans, First Narrows, through which all Vancouver harbour traffic must pass. In keeping with the flow of outgoing traffic under the bridge, Freddie Baker was favouring the north shore, while incoming vessels stayed close to the Stanley Park side, the south shore, and so, by common consent, created incoming and outgoing lanes through the narrow, crowded passage.

From the starboard side of the wheelhouse where Danny stood, it seemed they were too close to the north shore, so close that he could see the yellow sulphur accumulating at the end of a moving conveyor belt under the glare of the dock's bright lights.

"Aren't you a little . . . " he began, but was interrupted by Freddie Baker.

"Concerned about that boat coming toward us? Hell, it's small compared to ours. He'll keep his distance."

Ahead and to their port, the navigation lights of a small craft came closer. The *Etta Mae* passed safely through First Narrows and under the Lions Gate bridge, but just beyond the bridge, the outpouring current from the mouth of the Capilano River hit the *Etta Mae* broadside and began to push the boat toward Prospect Point and into the path of the oncoming vessel, visible now in the bridge's overhead lights as a tug boat bearing down on them with an unlighted barge in tow. The tug had unreeled too much tow line to properly control the barge in the flow of First Narrows, and the barge, no longer behind the tug but caught in the current, was now veering into mid-channel where it threatened to overtake the tug and smash apart the *Etta Mae*. Thousands of tons of limestone, loaded on the barge like two twin-peaked mountains, bore down on the *Etta Mae* and then, as they watched helplessly, the barge raced past to port, missing them by two yards as it plowed on through the night. As they passed, a deckhand stood illumined in their running lights on the outer walkway of the barge. He gripped the railing and stared down at the narrow margin of dark water eddying between them.

"I need a drink!" the woman said quietly.

She had given up the pretence of unpacking boxes, and was now searching in them for something specific.

"It's in here somewhere. I know it is." Her hands scrambled among the boxes and then were still, holding on to something. "Here it is!"

In the sweep of the radar screen light, he glimpsed her face, brown hair jutting out of a baseball cap, and a curious lopsided grin as she held a bottle by the neck and tilted it to her lips.

"I suppose you want to know where we're headed?" asked Lyle Thomas, as if by way of explanation for their near miss with disaster.

"Thing is, I don't know where we're going because our destination is always changing. Fish buyers follow the action, move with the fleet. Guess I'll just have to give you word on a need-to-know basis as I figure it out myself." He sipped from his coffee mug, holding on to it carefully so it wouldn't spill. "For now, stand by to take on ice and fuel tomorrow at Campbell River and then we'll shoot the narrows. I'm the mate, so you'll take orders from me. Freddie here is the skipper. You can deck, do some engine duty, and cook." He handed Danny the empty coffee mug. It would be his job to keep it filled.

The *Etta Mae* well out of the shelter of the harbour now, the weather changing, a south-east wind skimming the peaks of the waves, throwing spray, slamming the boat, Lyle Thomas stared into the rough breaking sea. "The hiring hall says you're familiar with this boat," he said. "That so?"

"Somewhat. How many you got for crew?" Danny asked.

"Freddie, me, and you. Just means we double up on things some, that's all. Marlene will help you in the galley. She's a great cook!" enthused Thomas. "And she pitches in whenever she can. Course having someone who knows the vessel like yourself is a bonus. We each do a little extra and everything runs smooth. Being a buyer of salmon we keep a cash payroll on board, so we can't be too careful. We like to have a weapon in plain view so no one turns funny on us during a deal."

But Danny still hadn't recovered from their near miss with the barge. "I can't believe you took us so close to the mouth of the Capilano River when it was clearly marked on the chart. You have all the charts, don't you?"

"Hell no!" said Thomas."Lookit this. Let me show you something way better than charts!"

He stood over an empty chart table, holding a piece of black plastic the dimensions of a thin three-ring binder which he opened, flicked a switch and the inside of the top cover which Danny now saw comprised a portable computer's LED screen lit up with colour.

Lyle Thomas's face hovered over the screen, his right hand worked the mouse, his finger clicked on the arrow. "See that. That's us." The arrow pointed at the crude shaped icon of a boat. "Right there. That's where we are at this moment."

"No. That's not us," said Danny. "That's not real. That's not us at all."

"Sure it is. It's us, and a laptop, and a little software, and a GPS. You know what a GPS is, don't you?"

Danny nodded. His daughter told him how the Global Positioning System sends a signal to a satellite that gives the exact co-ordinates of a ship's location.

"You should get one, Dad," she told him.

He hadn't seen his daughter in more than a year. How could a man without his own place even face his daughter, never mind afford expensive electronic equipment?

"Shows our exact location," Lyle Thomas insisted. "What I need to know is, are you with us? Are you up for it? Because if you're not, when we take on ice and fuel tomorrow, we can just drop you off with a day's pay and no hard feelings."

The pulsing green light swept the radar screen, illuminating a woman drinking tequila from a bottle, a skipper at the wheel with so little regard for common sailing directions he'd almost killed them before they got out of port, and a mate who didn't know where they were going. This was the crew of the *Etta Mae*. And himself, for he too was a part of the crew, and after all, who was he? An old man whose life on land had been a failure, who now, at the end of it, sought solace in the sea and a ship he had once known.

The boat was in open water now and he could only keep his balance by standing with his legs apart, moving with the pitch of the ship. A heaving wall of water rose ahead of them, blocking his vision. He held onto the railing and braced himself for the downward plunge of the bow.

"Yes," he said. "I'm on for the trip."

"Great," said Lyle Thomas. "Welcome aboard. You'd better turn in and get some sleep. We'll call you at six o'clock."

It was a dirty night but he would be safe in the forecastle and he began to make his way to that most forward, and, curiously, for him, his favourite part of the ship. He lay in his bunk, below deck, below the waterline. On the other side of the hull against which he lay, rushed the sea through which they were moving.

He turned off the small overhead lamp and in the darkness listened to the creak of the ship's timbers. All his life he had found it a comforting sound but tonight something was wrong. He couldn't sleep.

Tomorrow he would phone his daughter from the fuel dock in Campbell River, he told himself, turning in his bunk. First night out, he thought, unable to sleep. First night out, that's all.

Without Esther

A SMALL FOREST OF OLD GROWTH DOUGLAS FIR lines the inner cusp of the bay. The rocky soil causes the trees to grow slowly, and now, ragged and twisted with age, their scaled trunks and windswept branches stand above the waterline. Back from the shore, the trees grow healthy and tall. Only at the water's edge are they stunted and weather beaten. In the tidal bay itself, stands the pole shed on its black creosote pilings. Beneath it the tides come and go, while inside an old man moves about in what once had been his net shed. Now that there is no fishery, it has become his home.

Martin Gates slid the glass door open and stepping out onto the deck, settled into a cushioned wicker chair, an old man living out his last years at the edge of things, the sun lifting the smell of the beach into the afternoon summer air as he drifts in and out of memory.

. . . five years old and he stands in the back seat to see over his father's shoulder the sweep of headlights on the curve in the road ahead, the moving beams deflected and blocked by the giant trees that crowd to the road, their massive scaled black trunks blocking the headlight beams at every turn. The gravel bounces and clatters off the floorboards as his father drives through the night.

What is that noise? The droning noise waking him. Did he dream just now that he was in the back seat of his father's car in Cathedral Grove, or remember it? He must have dreamed it because he'd fallen asleep, awakened now by the snarl of a small engine somewhere in the distance, maybe the next bay over from his. And where was Esther?

Esther Gates, goddess of the geoducks, stalks the beach for the giant foot-long clams with their thick necks sticking out of the sand. Tiptoeing to them, for they sense the slightest disturbance and withdraw, she stoops to touch the thick, wrinkled protrusion poking out of the sand, and watches it shrink into its hole spraying an arc of sea water as it goes.

But not this one. Kneeling in the sand, she grasps its neck and now she must hold it with all her strength, hands buried beyond her wrists in the sand, she holds onto the geoduck and calls out across the beach, "Martin! Martin!"

He runs across the beach, clams tumbling in the bottom of his swinging pail, shovel over his shoulder. He drops the bucket and begins digging the sand around her hands, taking care not to nick them with the shovel blade.

All their life gathering food together, that summer day on this very beach so long ago when he dropped the shovel and they fell into each others arms, laughing in the sand. Where was she now, dammit? Where was Esther?

They went to school together in a town on the east coast of Vancouver Island where their fathers found work in the mill. Every afternoon except Sunday, traffic stopped so a ninety ton steam locomotive could cross main street pulling rail cars loaded with logs. Kids stood at the side of the rail tracks and watched the soul of their island pass in front of them as the clank and shunt and shudder of rail cars rolled the limbed, bucked and fallen giants into the mill. Out of its maw it spit lumber stacked on acres of asphalt to be shipped all over the world to rebuild in the post-war boom.

It was the largest sawmill in the British Empire. They were told so at school, and once it must have seemed so, for on a summer day the King and Queen of England received the people of the town on the golf course green.

Martin and Esther left the island only once on their honeymoon, and even then, they didn't really leave. He bought them a ferry ride across the straits because that was all he could afford, and why not, for in those days the crossings were slow, stately voyages aboard *Princess Alice*, *Princess Victoria*, and the last of the line, *Princess Elaine*.

They rented a stateroom and never came out of it. For in that enclosed space she was his ocean, undulant, rolling beneath him until they became very loose, and looking into her green eyes, he touched something deep inside her he had never felt before.

Knocking. Someone knocking at the door. There was a knocking at the door. "Excuse me sir," said the voice on the other side. "The ship has docked."

"But we're not getting off," said Martin. "We're just married. This is our honeymoon."

"Do you have round-trip tickets?" asked the purser.

"Yes, of course."

"Very well, then. We leave in an hour."

But where was Esther now? Everywhere. Kneeling on the forest floor to pick bright yellow-orange chanterelles bursting out of the green moss, or on the beach, but never with him here and now.

And there it was again. That sound. He tried to ignore it but it wouldn't go away, the drone of that distant engine. It was coming from the other side of the point, in the next bay over. He was sure of it.

All around him land had developed into high-end real estate; condos, resorts, gated communities, even a spa, and his own adjacent land had been assessed accordingly. His property taxes had now reached such exorbitant sums he could no longer pay them and hadn't for three consecutive years, not that he kept track. Esther took care of that kind of thing.

When Martin and Esther fished they lived on their boat, always intending to build a house in their forest when they retired but then the fishery closed and Martin moved into the net shed.

As long as it was a net shed, and he was just sleeping over in a cot, he was alright, but it was only a matter of time now before it was discovered he was living here.

Somehow Martin made it through the summer, his first summer without Esther, and in the fall he picked chanterelles in their forest, just as they had always done, but that was the problem, they had always done everything together, so now everywhere he went, and everything he did, reminded him of her.

In the forest ravens talked across the treetops in deep, resonant tones, and as he walked he felt the spring of the soft cushion of the forest floor under his feet. Dark brown bush tits the size of mice hopped about on the moss, and when he came nearer, ascended in a thronging cloud swirling above him in the forest canopy. But he was lost, lost without Esther in their forest.

He shut himself up in the net shed for the rainy season.

Waves from the high winter tide crashed against the shore and set beached logs loose. The rain on the roof kept him awake and the logs floating free in the bay bumped against the pilings under his shed. He was surrounded by water.

Some nights that winter the condo dwellers out on the point thought they saw from their windows a glimmer of light in the net shed but it seemed a world apart from theirs, and it was.

In February, the tide dropped in the afternoon and the beach began to show itself. The sun made steam rise from the soaked cedar shakes of the net shed roof and the fecund smell of the beach rose on the air for the first time that year.

Martin climbed down the ladder of the net shed onto the beach, unable to resist. He was alive! Striding across the sand carrying a clam bucket and a shovel, wading through the shallow pools, walking in the womb of the great mother of us all. He set his pail down in the sand, positioned his shovel, and sank the blade into the sand and at that exact moment remembered the same motion of the shovel in his hands that day on the beach so long ago when Esther . . . it was no good. It was no good without Esther. He dropped the shovel and slowly walked back to the net shed.

The sound from the point grew louder, insistent, troubling, for he knew what it was now. In the next bay over they were clearing land for an upscale gated community built on an age old Native burial site. The heavy equipment and earth-moving machine operators were instructed to place any human remains they found in a shed. Nothing could stop them and now they were expanding around the point and into his bay.

A full year had gone by and it was August again. When Martin looked up into the tops of the fir trees at this time of year, the thin supple new-growth uppermost branches bent with the weight of green fir cones that he picked when he was a boy. They were driven into the woods on a bus and climbed to the top of the trees to pick the cones for seed. A fifteen-year-old-boy poking his head above the bright green new growth branches of the forest canopy, a part of it, the mist that clings to the treetops, as he did then, held there by a rope, picking the cones into his sack.

The seed of future trees. If they planted new trees, they could cut down the old growth because there would always be more trees, a renewable resource, they said. But they cut them down faster than they could grow back; hundreds of years to grow to maturity, minutes to cut one down.

You hear a sound, a distant drone, like a mosquito, only deeper. Then the sound stops. A hundred and fifty foot giant fir slants out of the sky and crashes to the earth. It bounces when it hits the ground, the impact felt underfoot, and as it bounces the trunk does a kind of half-turn, and then the tree settles on its branches with a final rustle, dead. Repeated over and over, the same bounce, half-turn of the trunk, the final movement before it lies on its side, felled. One by one they were cutting down the trees on the point.

The whine and drone of the chainsaws so close now he felt the whole bay shudder with the impact of each felled tree. He knew then. He would not make it through another year, not without Esther.